# DEATH AS A LAST RESORT

# DEATH AS A LAST RESORT

Gwendolyn Southin

TouchWood
Editions

TouchWood Editions
www.touchwoodeditions.com

**Library and Archives Canada Cataloguing in Publication**
Southin, Gwendolyn
Death as a last resort / Gwendolyn Southin.
(A Margaret Spencer mystery)

ISBN 978-1-926741-02-4

I. Title. II. Series: Southin, Gwendolyn. Margaret
Spencer mystery.

PS8587.O978D423 2010      C813'.6      C2009-906897-4

Editor: Linda L. Richards
Proofreader: Christine Savage
Cover design: Tobyn Manthorpe

BRITISH COLUMBIA
ARTS COUNCIL
Supported by the Province of British Columbia

Canada Council    Conseil des Arts
for the Arts       du Canada

We gratefully acknowledge the financial support for our publishing
activities from the Government of Canada through the Canada Book Fund,
Canada Council for the Arts, and the province of British Columbia through
the British Columbia Arts Council and the Book Publishing Tax Credit.

**Mixed Sources**
Cert no. SW-COC-001271
© 1996 FSC

FSC

The interior of this book was produced on 100% post-consumer recycled
paper, processed chlorine free and printed with vegetable-based dyes.

The information in this book is true and complete to the best of the author's knowledge.
All recommendations are made without guarantee on the part of the author. The author
disclaims any liability in connection with the use of this information.

1 2 3 4 5 13 12 11 10

PRINTED IN CANADA

*Dedicated to my faithful readers who ask for more,
to those who are discovering Maggie and her adventures
for the first time, and as always, to my family and friends.*

## PROLOGUE
### 1943–Asyût, Egypt

The military police were everywhere. Not that the soldier thought they were following him, but it was a good idea to know exactly where they were.

It was dusk, and the narrow streets were still busy. Carpets were piled on the ground beside stalls where bolts of linens and cottons were displayed beside gaudy vases, figurines, faux relics and souvenirs. Scrawny goats and squawking chickens added to the general confusion of the other vendors hawking vegetables, dried fruits and spices. Women in traditional dress and a few on-leave soldiers fingered the merchandise, haggling loudly before making a purchase, moving from one stall to the next. Between them were small shops and cafés, their owners standing in open doorways to entice potential customers to come inside.

The soldier expertly stepped his way through the throng, dodging sellers and the hoards of ragged children clutching at his uniform. "*Imshi. Imshi.*" he yelled at them. Once free of the children, he glanced in both directions and then entered a small alleyway where he knocked on a scarred wooden door. The woman who answered wore a white linen robe and the traditional hyab so that her hair and shoulders were completely covered.

"*Salam alekum,*" he greeted her.

"*Wa alekum es salam,*" she answered, carefully keeping her eyes downcast.

"*Bititkalimy Englizee?*" he asked hopefully.

"A little."

"I," he touched his chest, "to meet Akhum." He handed her a sealed envelope. "Give to Akhum."

Taking the envelope, she moved to the back of the shop and pushed her way through a curtain of brightly coloured beads. He could hear a rapid exchange in an unfamiliar dialect before the beads swung abruptly aside, and a thin-faced man in his late fifties wearing a white jalabiya appeared.

"*Salam alekum.* And how is your respected father?" The man was holding the envelope.

"He sends you greetings, Akhum."

"Come through. First we have coffee. You follow in your father's footsteps, then?" Akhum said as he poured thick coffee into small cups. "He was in British Army when first we met."

"He told me you are the best."

Akhum bowed to acknowledge the compliment. "I have only a few pieces that I can show you now." Rising, he opened a cupboard and withdrew a cloth-covered packet. "Only a few pieces, as I said, but exquisite." He unrolled the packet and the lamplight glinted on the turquoise and beaded necklace and bracelet.

The soldier gasped as he picked up the ancient jewellery. "How old are they?"

"They're from the tomb of Maiherpri—Eighteenth Dynasty."

"How much?"

The haggling began . . .

# CHAPTER ONE

Margaret Spencer was having a terrific day until she found the man frozen in the snow.

She had felt that she was at long last getting the hang of this cross-country ski business. It was all a matter of rhythm, she thought. She leaned to the left to negotiate the next bend in the trail and promptly skidded straight into her partner, Nat Southby, sending both of them flying into the snow-laden bushes.

"Wow!" he gasped as he untangled himself. "And just as I was going to compliment you for catching on so quickly."

Maggie's reply was a scoop of fresh snow that hit him on the neck with a whomp. "No need to be cocky just because you've been skiing since you were a kid," she told him. "And," she added," if you hadn't stopped right there in the middle of the trail, I'd have been just fine." Then she started to laugh. "I must admit that I wish I'd taken this up long ago." Struggling to get back on her feet, she glanced up at the sky. "It's starting to snow again. I guess we'd better get back before it gets any worse."

"I guess," he replied reluctantly as he offered her a hand. "There's an easy trail down just ahead," he added. "We'll make for that."

Maggie and Nat, the owners of a Vancouver detective agency, had just returned from a snowy Christmas and New Year's in Quebec where Maggie had enjoyed her first experience with cross-country skiing. Now, back in Vancouver on the last day of their vacation, they were trying out their new skis on Hollyburn Mountain.

"Lead on," she said as she slid her skis to and fro to free the lumps of ice that had formed under them.

Nat waited until a family of four had passed—even the littlest one seemed to be an expert. He pulled on his gloves and pushed back onto the trail. "I'll take it slow," he teased, "so that you can keep up."

"I'll get you for that remark later," she shouted to his departing back.

Fifteen minutes later he came to an abrupt stop at the entrance to a narrow trail. "This leads down to the car park."

"What's *that*, Nat?" Maggie asked as she caught up to him. She pointed with her ski pole to the right.

He glanced up the side of the mountain that was just visible through the sparse trees. "I don't remember that clearing," he said. "And by the look of it, I'd say it's been cut quite recently."

"What a pity," Maggie answered. "It'll take years before the trees grow back."

"I heard that some company was going to open several more ski runs up here," he continued, "but why clear such a big area?" He sighed. "I guess that's progress for you."

"We should come back and have a look when the snow's gone," Maggie answered.

"You won't want to see it without the snow. That's the only thing that's hiding the mess the loggers have probably left behind. Come on, let's go. I'm starving."

Maggie was tiring as she manoeuvred her skis around the final bends on the downhill trail. Then she missed one altogether and fell headlong into a snowbank. She righted herself and then rested a moment, with her back against a snow-covered log. When she realized that Nat would now be far ahead of her, she dug her poles into the snow to get back onto her feet. But her weight shifted the log and she found herself falling back, arms flailing.

"Drat!" Sitting upright again, she slipped the loops of her ski poles from her wrists, unlatched her skis and rolled over onto her knees, dislodging a thin layer of snow from the log. That was when she saw the frozen fingers on the hand that emerged from the snow. "Oh my God," she breathed. The hand seemed to beckon to her.

"Nat!" Maggie screamed, scrambling on hands and knees to get away from the grotesque fingers.

"I'm coming," he yelled as he turned and began slogging his way up the trail. "Just stay put."

When he reached her, he found her standing in the middle of the trail, apparently unhurt. "What's the matter?" he asked.

Her answer was to point down.

"Bloody hell!" He kicked off his skis and knelt to brush the rest of the snow from the log Maggie had leaned against during her brief rest. It wasn't a log at all, but a man. A man who was most definitely dead. And frozen stiff.

Maggie's voice quivered. "His head's covered in blood. Do you think he had a fall or something?"

Nat looked all around, then shook his head. "No broken branches, and he's sort of tucked behind those bushes. Besides, he's not wearing skis . . . or ski clothes." He got to his feet. "We'd better get some help."

"You can ski faster than I can," Maggie answered. "You go and I'll wait here."

He shook his head. "You're not staying here by yourself. It's already getting dark."

"But we can't just leave him." She peered back up the slope. "There's bound to be someone else coming down the trail."

"I doubt it. We're probably the last on the mountain." Nat

thought for a moment. "Besides, by the look of him, he's been dead for quite a while. Another hour won't make any difference."

Maggie shivered as the cold wind blew the thickening snow into their faces. "I do hope the police won't want us to come back up here tonight."

"One of us will have to come back, I guess," Nat answered. "You got a hanky or something that we can tie on the bushes to mark the spot?"

"Here, take this," she said, pulling off the red silk scarf that she was wearing and handing it to him.

It seemed an eternity before they reached the parking lot, where they piled their skis into Nat's old Chevy and drove to the nearest phone booth, which was outside a coffee shop.

"They're sending someone," Nat said after he replaced the receiver, "but they want us to wait back at the parking lot." He started toward the store. "I'll get them to refill our Thermos, okay?"

They drove back to the deserted lot and huddled close to the Chevy's feeble heater while they sipped their coffee and waited. Finally, a car with the West Vancouver Police insignia on the door drew up beside them. Nat reluctantly pulled himself away from Maggie's warmth and got out to meet the two officers who emerged.

"You the one found the stiff?"

Nat nodded. "I suppose you want me to go up the trail with you?"

"Afraid so. How far is it?" By this time the second officer had opened the trunk of the police car and was busy lighting a gas lantern. "I'm Sergeant Murray and this is my partner, Constable Jefferies."

Nat nodded acknowledgment. "Southby," he said. "It's a half mile or so up the trail."

"Let's get going, then. You get to carry the lantern."

Nat opened the passenger door of his car. "Will you be okay here on your own, Maggie?"

"I didn't know you had someone with you." Jefferies walked over to peer into Nat's car. "You saw the dead man, too?"

"Yes," Maggie replied miserably. "I found him." All she could think of was being home in her own house by her own fire.

"Don't go anywhere," Jefferies ordered.

Maggie felt like asking where the hell he thought she would go, but she watched in silence as the three of them, Nat leading the way with the lantern, trudged through the snow and disappeared into the entrance to the dark trail. She took another sip of the now cold coffee, curled herself up on the seat and, hoping she wasn't going to freeze as solid as the corpse, waited.

It was a good hour later before she saw the wavering light coming back down the trail, but she waited until they had reached the car park before opening the door and slogging her way through the deepening snow to meet them.

"Did you find him?" Maggie asked.

"Yeah. Can't move him until the coroner and homicide get here," Murray answered. "Constable Jeffries will wait here until they arrive. In the meantime, I want you two to follow me to the station."

Luckily the police station was only a ten-minute drive from the car park, and at least there was hot coffee. Murray took notes as he led them through their finding the body.

"And you're sure you don't know this man? I mean it seems funny that you stumble over a body and you're in the private detective business."

"We've told you twice that we don't know him," Nat answered testily. "Now please let me take Mrs. Spencer home. We are both very tired and very cold."

Murray nodded. "You can go after you've signed a written statement. Be prepared to come in if we need you."

BUT NAT AND MAGGIE heard nothing more from the West Vancouver police, and apart from a short item in the newspaper a couple of days later that said the body of an unidentified middle-aged man had been found on the mountain on January 6, the story garnered little attention from the media. The following week was so hectic they completely forgot about the body in the snow. Nat had gone ahead with his plans for expansion by renting the empty office next to the one they already had. It was Wednesday before the builders left after renovating and painting the new room and fitting a door to the original reception area, which was to become the sole domain of Henny, their girl Friday. There was dust everywhere, tempers were short and everything seemed to take twice as long as usual to get accomplished.

Henny Vandermeer, five foot eight, in her mid-forties and a lover of hand-knitted garments and stout shoes, had ruled the agency since taking over Maggie's job as Girl Friday a couple of years back. She was having a hard time accepting all the changes. "I stay here, ja?" she asked for what seemed the tenth time that morning.

"Yes, Henny," Maggie answered as patiently as possible. "Nat is using the new office. I've got his old one and you will stay right where you are."

"This mess is going to be gone soon, ja?"

"We should be almost straight by the end of the week. Nat's new carpet is being put down tomorrow."

"And my files?" Henny asked, pointing to the boxes piled in the corner.

"I'll give you a hand putting them into those nice new cabinets this afternoon," Maggie answered. "And you get to keep them along with the coffee pot and the coat rack."

"But where is my telephone?"

Maggie sighed. "The new phones will be connected later today, and then you'll be able to put through any calls for me or Nat." She turned as footsteps sounded outside the door. "That's probably the phone people now."

But it was the sign writer to add Maggie's name to Nat's on the door. After he had done his job and departed, Maggie stood on the landing and gazed at his handiwork.

*It's really happened. I'm actually a partner.* "Southby and Spencer, Private Investigators," she said out loud, just to see how it sounded. *And not: Maggie Spencer, housewife.*

She was so preoccupied that she didn't hear the ancient elevator grinding its way upward or its door opening just down the hall, so she was startled when an overdressed woman about her own age pushed past her. But Maggie's glance took in the freshly coiffed peroxide hair, the liberal use of mascara and, rather enviously, the beautifully manicured nails.

"Can I help you?" she asked.

The woman paused with her hand on the doorknob to look Maggie up and down before she marched into the office. "I want to speak to my husband," she announced to Henny. When a confused Henny only stared at her, she repeated, "My husband, Nat Southby."

Henny gasped. "Mr. Nat is married?"

Then Maggie remembered where she had seen the woman before. Nat had shown her a couple of old photographs of himself and his wife Nancy before their divorce.

"Is he in?" Nancy Southby checked her wristwatch. "I was hoping he'd take me out for lunch."

"He'll be out until two," Maggie said, following the woman into the office. "I'll tell him you called."

"No need. I'll be back before then." She opened the door and then pointed at the sign. "Who's this Spencer person?"

"I'm Maggie Spencer."

"Huh! I read about you in the newspapers. Didn't take you long to get your hooks into him."

It was all Maggie could do not to reply, but by the time Nat returned a half hour later, she was ready to explode. "Your ex-wife came in a short while ago," she said, leaving Henny to finish sorting the files and leading the way into her office.

"Nancy?" he said, following her.

"Apparently she read about me when our last case was written up in the newspapers, and now she seems to think I've got my hooks well and truly into you."

"What the hell did she want?"

"Lunch for starters, but she's coming back around two to tell you the rest of it," she answered sweetly.

"If she thinks I'm giving her more money," he thundered, "she's got another think coming." He stormed out, heading for his own office.

Maggie smiled as she closed her door quietly behind him.


"IS HE IN?" NANCY asked, shedding her Persian lamb coat as she made a beeline for Nat's office.

"You wait!" Henny interposed her bulk between the woman and Nat's door, ready to defend her boss. "I'll see if he is busy, ja?"

"Don't bother," she answered, pushing Henny aside.

"I'm sorry, Mr. Nat," Henny said miserably. "I ask her to wait."

"It's okay, Henny." He turned to his ex. "What is it this time, Nancy?"

"You got any decent coffee in this place?"

"I'll get coffee," Henny answered, closing the door behind her and making straight for Maggie's office. "She's back again."

"Who's back again?" Maggie asked, looking up from her work.

"Mr. Nat's old wife."

"I wonder what she wants?"

"That's what Mr. Nat ask her. But she wants coffee . . . now."

"OKAY, NANCY," NAT SAID. "What gives?"

"The police told my friend Jacquelyn Dubois that it was you that found her husband dead on that mountain," she said.

"Not exactly. My partner, Mrs. Spencer, found him."

"And now this has come out," she carried on as if he hadn't spoken and waved a newspaper at him. "Yesterday's paper. Have you read it?"

"No," he answered, bewildered. "Should I have?"

"Here, read it." And she thrust the article in front of him.

The Sun has learned that the body of a man in his late fifties that was discovered by two unidentified skiers on Saturday, January 6, on Hollyburn Mountain, was the late Maurice Dubois. He had been reported missing by his wife, Jacquelyn, on January 3 when she returned from a vacation in Montreal. He had been on a fishing trip with a few friends at St. Clare Cove Resort and Marina, situated in Pender Harbour on the Sunshine Coast, when he disappeared.

Dubois owned a successful logging company operating on the Lower Mainland, Sechelt Inlet and Vancouver Island and was a business associate of Schaefer's Lumber and Building Supplies in North Vancouver. Mrs. Dubois was too distraught to be interviewed, but according to a close acquaintance, she was completely mystified why her husband's body was found on Hollyburn Mountain.

When this reporter enquired the cause of death, he was informed that the autopsy showed the death was from a severe blow to the head.

"So what has this to do with me?" Nat demanded.

"Jacquelyn wants to know who murdered him." She paused for a moment before bursting out, "So I gave her your name."

"Why? The police are taking care of it."

"She doesn't trust the cops too much. She wants an independent inquiry."

"But why me?"

"You're supposed to be some kind of detective, aren't you? So," she added, "when can she come and see you?"

There was a tap on the door and Henny came bustling in with two cups of coffee and one huge, lumpy cookie, which she pointedly placed on a napkin in front of her boss. "Anything else, Mr. Nat?"

"Take a look in the appointment book and see if Maggie and I have a free hour tomorrow or Friday."

"Do you need to bring *that woman* into this?"

"*That woman*, Nancy, is my partner. And we always cooperate on big cases, especially a murder."

Henny reappeared at the door, book in hand. "Nothing until eleven on Monday morning, Mr. Nat."

He looked enquiringly at Nancy.

"I'll call her and find out. Pass your phone over."

"There's a phone in the outer office," Nat replied curtly. "Then if your friend wants that slot, Henny can book her into it."

Grabbing the fur coat that she had flung over her chair, Nancy stormed out of Nat's office, slammed the door, settled behind Henny's desk and picked up the phone. "Jacquelyn," she said into the phone, "can you make Monday at eleven?"

*Now I have to break the good news to Maggie*, Nat thought as he listened to the muted voice of his ex-wife in the outer office. But a shout of dismay, some blue language and several thumps made him rush to the door. Nancy, in the act of marching out of the office, had collided with two men entering from the corridor, staggering under the weight of several heavy boxes containing telephones, coils of wire and other equipment that were now scattered over the floor of the office. The two men were gaping with astonishment and Nancy was livid.

"Watch where you're going, you idiots!" she shouted at them as she bent to retrieve her handbag, and she slammed out of the room without a backward glance.

"What was all that about?" the installer asked Maggie when she appeared in her office doorway. "You'll have to pay for new telephones if they're broken, you know," he added.

Nat stomped back into his office and slammed the door. Maggie would have liked to do the same, but she waited patiently while the installer inspected everything for damage.

Henny watched apprehensively as he unpacked the console onto her desk. "All those buttons. How do I know which one to push?"

"I'm sure this gentleman will explain everything," Maggie answered. "It'll be quite easy, you'll see."

"But . . ."

Maggie escaped into her own office, shut the door firmly behind her, drew some legal papers that a courier had delivered earlier in the day toward her, and tried to concentrate.

But her peace was short-lived. "The telephone man wants to come in here next," Henny said, poking her head into the room.

"Can't he do Nat's office? I'm busy."

"The man has come to put down the carpet in Mr. Nat's office."

"But he wasn't supposed to come until tomorrow."

"He said he has spare time today."

"I give up."

By the sound of the raised voices emanating from Nat's office, Maggie didn't think he and the carpet layer were getting along too well either. It was obviously time to take Nat out for an afternoon break.

"I don't understand about buttons," Henny yelled as Maggie headed toward his door.

"You the boss?" the telephone man asked in exasperation.

Maggie nodded.

"It's quite simple to use. Let me explain."

"Can you wait for just a few minutes?" she asked.

"Lady," he replied testily, "I have two more installations to do this afternoon . . ."

Maggie was beginning to wonder if the new Southby and Spencer Agency would ever achieve some kind of normalcy.

## CHAPTER TWO

The office was quiet. The telephone system had been installed, Henny had departed for home after Maggie assured her she would explain all the buttons in the morning, the carpet man had left, and she and Nat were sitting in her office going over the day's events.

"You'd better read this," Nat said, sliding the folded newspaper towards Maggie. "I wonder why it's taken the cops so long to identify him?"

Maggie picked up the newspaper and read the article. "You're right. It's been two weeks since we found the body." She handed the paper back to him. "It was easy to see that he'd been bashed on the head." She couldn't help giving a shiver. "Of course, it was getting quite dark when we discovered him."

"I wonder why Mrs. Dubois wasn't at the resort with her husband?" Nat mused.

"Perhaps she prefers the city life," Maggie answered. "Not everyone is into a log-fires-antlers-on-the-wall kind of vacation."

"We'll probably find out when we interview her on Monday." He stood up to leave, then turned back. "By the way, that was a good piece of work you did on that housebreaking case."

"It didn't take much to figure out that the boyfriend was helping himself to the family silver as well as the daughter's charms," she answered. "Henny's already typed the report up for me so we can bill Smedley and Company." The publicity from their last big cases meant that their agency was now doing quite a bit of work for a number of law firms, Smedley, Smedley and Dawson being one of them.

"Come on. Grab your purse and let's go and splurge our hard-earned money on a steak at Monty's."

Maggie didn't need any prodding.

JACQUELYN DUBOIS WAS SMALL, slim, dark and very young—probably in her early twenties. She was dressed in deep mourning—black pillbox hat with a small veil, black dress, shoes, stockings and handbag. The black mink draped over her shoulders and the fingers covered in rings spoke of money.

"You know, it's early days yet, Mrs. Dubois. Perhaps you should give the police a little more time," Nat suggested when the three of them were seated.

"Maurice had no time for *les cops*," Jacquelyn Dubois answered, her accent giving away her Quebecois heritage. "And I think there was . . . how do you say . . . funny business going on in his death."

"Funny business?" Maggie asked. "When was the last time you saw your husband?"

"At my papa's house in Montréal. Then Maurice flew back here to the Coast on the December 27."

"Any reason why you didn't come with him?" Nat asked.

Jacquelyn's beautiful little face registered disgust. "Fishing camps do not appeal."

"Did he call you from the lodge?"

"*Non*." She took a lace-edged hankie out of her handbag and gently dabbed her eyes. "I called the resort when he didn't come home, and they told me he had left on the previous Saturday."

"Did your husband know the others up at the lodge?" Maggie asked.

"Some. They are . . . how do you say . . . business associates."

"To do with his logging operation?" Nat asked.

"*Non, non.* He has an interest in the St. Clare Cove Resort. He wants . . . wanted to subdivide and build big houses there."

"And the guests were potential customers?" Maggie asked.

"*Oui.*"

"Did you know any of them?" Nat asked.

Jacquelyn Dubois shook her head. "As I say, it was business. I know nothing about business. Maurice always tell me . . ." she paused and blushed, "not to worry my pretty little head. Now I wish I had asked questions."

"What about his partner?" Nat asked, looking down at the notes he'd made earlier. "Arnold Schaefer?"

"He and his wife are, how do you say . . . stuffy."

"What about family, Mrs. Dubois?" Maggie asked. "Children?"

"Maurice and I are only married for six months. But he has a son and daughter from his previous marriages."

"Marriages?"

"Oui, he was married two times before."

"And they all live in Quebec?" Nat asked.

"*Non, non.* They live here in Vancouver. René used to work at logging for Maurice, but he was no good." She shrugged. "Now he works somewhere . . ." She waved a hand dismissively. "And has his own apartment. Isabelle, she is at some kind of school— hair-dressing or something like that."

"So she doesn't live with you."

"*Non-non.* She lives with her mother." Then, twisting her handkerchief in her well-manicured hands, she looked piteously up at Nat. "So it is the estate, you understand. I must get it settled.

But, of course, I must know who killed my dear, dear Maurice in this . . . awful way, oui."

Nat, who was not easily fooled by the 'poor-little-me' act and could see that the girl, at least twenty years younger than her deceased husband, was probably more concerned about what the estate was worth than the man's murder, asked, "Who is the main beneficiary of your husband's will?"

She hesitated for a moment before answering. "Naturally I am, but what is money if I don't have my dear Maurice?" She dabbed her eyes again before adding, "His children get five thousand each."

"I see. Have the police released the body?" he asked.

"He is in the Mountain View Funeral Home," she said, dabbing her eyes once more. "My Maurice look so peaceful and I will give him a beautiful funeral."

"And where will that be?" Nat asked.

"Two o'clock on Thursday at Holy Rosary Cathedral. You know it?"

Nat nodded as he made a notation on his yellow pad.

"And you will find the maniac who kill him?"

"If you're sure that's what you really want," Nat answered, "but it could be very expensive for you."

She stood and gathered up her coat and purse. "You want me to sign something?"

"Maggie will take you to her office and explain our retainer system and our contract. Then if you still wish us to take on the case, she will have you sign a contract."

"Well," Maggie said, after she had shown their new client out, "are you really up to tackling such a young and beautiful widow?"

"I've a bad feeling about all this, and it's not just because Nancy's mixed up in it."

"So have I," Maggie answered. "I mean, why did Dubois leave that fishing lodge up the coast and end up dead on the mountain? And," she added, "where do we start on this one?"

"First, we'll get Henny to set up appointments for us."

"I suggest that the partner, Arnold Schaefer, should be at the top of the list and that we both go to see him," Maggie said. "You know . . . first impressions . . ."

"And presumably he can give us a list of everyone who was at the fishing lodge." He reached over to his console. "Henny, how would you like to bring in your notebook?"

ARNOLD SCHAEFER'S SECRETARY informed them that her boss was out of town until Wednesday and the only time she could fit them in that day would be at ten o'clock. She didn't know who had been up at the lodge with him but said she would ask as soon as her boss came in.

"I've a hunch this is going to be a long investigation," Nat said, replacing the receiver. "So how about we have a relaxing dinner out tonight?"

"I've a much better idea," Maggie answered with a smile. "How about a leisurely dinner at my place—candles and the works? Six o'clock?"

"Ahh . . . I especially like the idea of *the works*."

OSCAR, THE SPANIEL CROSS left to Maggie by her aunt, greeted her at the front door with his lead in his mouth. As she bent to pat his head, she noticed there was a fresh scratch on his nose. "Where's your pal?" she asked in trepidation. Things hadn't gone too well since she had brought him home to live with her and Emily, the white cat that had once belonged to the elderly victim in her first-ever murder case.

But when Maggie checked the kitchen and living room, she

found that everything was in place. Even the rugs! After picking up pieces of china each time she came home, she had removed her few remaining ornaments to safer places. But tonight Emily was sitting on the windowsill, fastidiously washing, and Maggie was sure she had a satisfied look on her face.

"You've put Oscar in his place, I see."

The cat ignored the remark and went on washing.

Nat, always on time for a meal, arrived with the wine. Oscar was so pleased to see him that he nearly sent him and the bottle flying. "Hey, watch it, dog," Nat said, nudging the exuberant animal away with his foot.

Laughing, Maggie grabbed Oscar's collar with one hand and the bottle with the other. "Well, do I get a kiss for saving you from this ferocious beast?"

"You bet! But only after you've safely put that bottle down."

Nat had become so much a part of Maggie's life that she couldn't imagine what it would be like without him. She realized that their families, friends and business acquaintances knew that their relationship was more than platonic. This fact must have been on Nat's mind, too, as after the supper dishes had been done and they were sitting on either side of the fireplace, he said, "Heard anything from Harry lately?"

Maggie and Harry, a lawyer for Snodgrass, Crumbie and Spencer, had been separated for three years now, but Harry still lived in the hope that she would see the error of her ways, give up her job with the detective agency, and return to their family home.

"No. But Barbara called a few days ago and said that he had been made vice-president in the firm. He deserves it really," she added. "He works very hard for them."

"Isn't it time you divorced him, Maggie?"

"You know that it's out of the question," she answered.

"Neither Harry nor I would ever collude by staging a sham adultery. I just couldn't do that to him. And I'm not about to have you named as co-respondent, either." She was silent for a moment, thinking about her estranged husband. Even though Harry's picky ways had irritated her until she had to leave him, she still felt some loyalty to him. After all, he was the father of her two daughters and she had been married to the man for over twenty-five years.

"Does he know that you're a partner in the business now?"

Maggie shook her head. "I haven't even told the girls yet. Guess I'm waiting for the right moment."

"Maggie," he replied, standing up, "you've got to *find* the right moment." He walked over to the closet and took his coat off the hanger. "And I mean not only the partnership but the situation between you and Harry." He bent over her chair and kissed her on the forehead. "I'll see you in the morning."

"You're not staying over?" she asked, feeling a little disappointed.

"No. Got some things I have to do."

Maggie sat thinking for quite a while after he had gone, and she realized that deep down she didn't want to confront Harry about a divorce. *Why can't things just go on as they are?*

## CHAPTER THREE

It was quite easy for Maggie and Nat to find Schaefer's Lumber and Building Supplies in North Vancouver. As they drove through the gates, they could see that the yard was humming with workmen driving trucks and forklifts—it looked like a very busy and lucrative place. The lovely smell of wood that drifted from the planning mill and the drying kilns stayed with them in the cold air as they parked outside the cedar-shingled office.

"Mr. Schaefer will just be a moment," the dark-haired receptionist informed them. "He's running a bit late." Then she added in a whisper, "He's on the phone with that Mrs. Dubois, helping her with the funeral arrangements."

"That's tomorrow, isn't it?" Maggie asked.

The receptionist nodded. "Isn't it awful about Mr. Dubois's murder? Such a nice man," she ran on. "Who would want to murder him?"

"Have you worked here long?" Maggie asked.

"Six months. But he was always so nice to me."

"Mr. Southby . . . ?" A short, red-faced man with a decided paunch stood in the doorway of one of the offices.

"And this is my partner, Mrs. Spencer," Nat filled in.

"Partner?" he said. Maggie could see him sifting this bit of information before extending his hand toward Nat. "Arnold

Schaefer. Well, I suppose you'd better come in." And he led the way into his office. "What on earth does that woman want to employ a private dick for?" he demanded and then, without waiting for an answer, he eased down into his ox-blood leather chair and continued, "Waste of money. Let the cops do their work. That's what we pay our taxes for." He indicated that the two of them should sit. "And she's even got me doing the funeral arrangements," he said disgustedly.

"Are you talking about Mrs. Dubois?" Maggie asked.

Schaefer continued as if she hadn't spoken. "Why doesn't she get that lazy René to help? He's left me in a terrible mess."

"Maurice Dubois has left you in a mess?" Maggie asked, feeling thoroughly confused.

"As if I haven't got enough on my plate with the lumberyard and logging operation and then—wouldn't you know—my accountant up and left," he continued, ignoring Maggie's question.

"Mr. Dubois was a partner in the firm?" Nat asked.

"Not really. We had a working contract. His logging companies supply . . . or should I say *supplied* . . . lumber for my yard."

"You were one of the guests at St. Clare Cove over New Year's?" Maggie asked.

Hardly glancing at her, he turned to Nat to answer. "Yes. Maurice had this hare-brained scheme of pulling all those disgusting cabins down and building something he called condominiums there. As if anyone in their right mind would buy anything that far up the coast."

"So you were all invited up to see the property," Nat said.

"You knew the others who were there?" Maggie asked.

He hesitated for a moment before actually answering her question. "I'd met one or two of them before." He looked toward the door as the secretary came in holding a sheet of paper. "Put it on the desk, girl. Don't just stand there."

"Any idea who would want to murder him?"

"Maybe a jealous husband? He's always had a roving eye. Anyway," he continued maliciously, "he was certainly enjoying himself at the lodge—and without his missus, I might add."

"Do you know what Jacquelyn did before she married Dubois?" Maggie asked.

"A dancer or something like that. Like all the bits of fluff that Dubois chased."

"So was he enjoying himself with some of the other wives at the lodge? Anyone in particular?"

"He flirted with them, but there was a barmaid . . ."

"Did he go up to Pender Harbour by car?" Maggie interrupted.

"He went up with me."

"What day was that?" Nat asked.

"Thursday. Picked him up at the airport. He was in Montreal over Christmas."

"So you picked him up on December 27."

"Yeah. Then we caught that damned Blackball ferry from Horseshoe Bay."

"And what day did he disappear?"

"Must have been sometime on the Saturday while we were out fishing."

"Did you have time to make us a list of those at the lodge?" Nat asked.

"That's what the girl just brought in," he said, passing the typed sheet over to Nat. "But they won't know any more than I do." Just then the phone rang and the two of them sat waiting while Arnold Schaefer reamed out the caller. "What do ya mean the truck is stuck in the mud?" he yelled. "That load was supposed to be here by nine today. I don't care *how* you do it, just get the bloody thing out." He slammed down the receiver and stood up.

"Can't get good help anywhere these days," he muttered. "You can let yourselves out."

"Did you all go out fishing that day?" Maggie asked, getting to her feet.

"All the men. The wives did whatever you women do."

A tall, blond, moustached man sitting in the reception area looked up expectantly as they left Schaefer's office.

"If he's applying for that vacant accounting job," Nat said as he slid behind the wheel, "he's going to need lots of stamina."

"I wouldn't work for that man for any money," Maggie said as they drove out of the gates. "He's a real bully."

"His wife must be a saint," Nat said, laughing. "But I think we've just got to find time to make it to that funeral tomorrow."

THERE WERE NO PARKING spaces left near the Holy Rosary Cathedral on Richards Street, so by the time Nat had manoeuvred the old Chevy into a tight spot on Homer and they had walked back, the church was full and the coffin had arrived at the impressive front doors. One of the black-dressed ushers solemnly held back the latecomers while the chief mourners jockeyed for the place of honour behind the coffin. Besides Jacquelyn there was one other heavily veiled woman who was trying to push a dark-haired young man in his early twenties to the front, but she hadn't reckoned on Jacquelyn, who hissed, "What the hell are you doing here?"

"René is Maurice's only son and he has the right to be first behind the coffin," the other woman hissed back, "and I am *still* his wife in the eyes of the Church."

But Jacquelyn, lace handkerchief at the ready, leaned on a grim-faced Arnold Schaefer and pushed into the lead.

Maggie was hoping to see the outcome of the confrontation, but Nat led her into the church. There they waited for the usher to take them to a seat, but he was caught up in an argument with another two heavily veiled women.

"We have to be in the front pew," the elder of the two announced in a loud voice.

"The front pew is for family, madam," the usher said quietly.

"We *are* family," the woman retorted. "Isabelle is Maurice's daughter." And pushing the poor man aside, she sailed down the aisle, dragging a very reluctant teenaged girl behind her, and they ensconced themselves in the family pew.

The organ music suddenly quieted and the usher, with a look of panic on his face, grabbed Maggie's arm, rushed her and Nat to the front and practically pushed them into two seats near the choir stalls.

"At least we can see what's going on," Maggie whispered.

"Shh!" Nat hissed as the incense bearer and the priest entered the nave, followed by the coffin with a huge ornate floral arrangement on it and three pallbearers walking on each side. Jacquelyn Dubois, leaning on a now obviously embarrassed Arnold Schaefer, sobbed daintily into her black-edged handkerchief. But Maggie noticed that the tears dried up very quickly when Jacquelyn realized that wife number two and daughter were sitting in her place and wife number one and son were coming up fast behind her.

Arnold Schaefer bent over wife number two. "Please move along, Edith," he said, but Edith Dubois wasn't about to be jockeyed out of her spot. She totally ignored him.

"Get out of my seat!" Jacquelyn hissed. Then realizing that Edith was not going to move and that the congregation was agog at this sudden drama, she furiously climbed over the huge tapestry hassock and sat down—only to have to get up again as wife number one and son pushed past mother and daughter and then Jacquelyn to sit down on her left. Jacquelyn looked wildly about for Schaefer, but he had quickly left the arena and crossed the aisle to sit with his well-dressed wife, who was in a wheelchair.

Maggie was hoping there would be more fireworks, but Jacquelyn, realizing that she had been out-manoeuvred and that she was playing to a church full of people, sank onto her knees on the hassock, doing a fairly good imitation of the exhausted widow overcome with grief.

The funeral, accompanied by a full mass, droned on. The priest, who obviously had never met the deceased, extolled all his wonderful qualities as a husband, father and breadwinner. "I wonder if he knows that there are three Mrs. Duboises sitting in the front pew?" Maggie whispered to Nat.

"He's probably getting a huge donation from the merry widow," he whispered back, "so doesn't care how many wives there are."

The long service finally came to an end, but Maggie and Nat waited until most of the congregation had filed out of the church before following the procession to the cemetery.

IT WAS A BEAUTIFUL winter day, and the 106 landscaped acres of Mountain View Cemetery on Fraser Street were at their best. "What a gorgeous place," Maggie breathed as they parked the old Chevy.

"You haven't been here before?" Nat asked, surprised. "All my relatives are buried here."

"Look," Maggie said, pointing. "The hearse has arrived, and there's all the family. Come on." She grabbed Nat's hand.

"But apart from the three merry widows," Nat panted as he followed her, trying to get his breath, "we really don't know who to look for." He stopped short. "Isn't that old George over there?" George Sawasky, a detective sergeant in the Vancouver Police homicide squad, had been Nat's partner when he had been in the force.

"He's seen us. Why don't you go and have a word with him," Maggie replied, stopping beside a huge maple tree. "I'll watch the show from here."

"Good idea!"

Maggie watched him walk toward his old friend before she too moved a little closer to the circle of people around the grave. She stopped beside a woman, probably in her early thirties and dressed in a mid-calf, dark grey wool coat, standing apart from the others.

"I can't believe dear Maurice has gone," the woman said suddenly. "He was so full of life." She wiped her eyes. "And to think that we were with him just a few days before he died."

"Had you known him long?" Maggie asked, pulling up her coat collar against a sudden gust of cold wind as it swept across the open cemetery.

"Quite a few years," she replied. She attempted to push a few stray strands of auburn hair back under her black felt hat before continuing. "He was a real ball of fire before that Jacquelyn got her . . ." She stopped suddenly. "I mean, before he married Jacquelyn."

Maggie had a sudden thought. "You didn't happen to be up at the fishing lodge with him over New Year's?"

"We were, as a matter of fact," she answered. "That's my husband, Robert, over there. He was one of the pall bearers." She pointed to a tall, stern-looking man standing beside another couple. "Why?"

"My partner and I are looking into Maurice Dubois's death."

"Are you the police?"

"No," Maggie answered. "Private investigators. Look, I've a list that Mr. Schaefer gave me. Would it be possible for you to help me match up some names with the people here?"

"I'm not sure . . . perhaps you should ask Robert."

"And your name is . . . ?" Maggie said as she whipped the list out of her handbag.

"Stella, Stella Edgeworthy." Reluctantly, she took the list from Maggie's hands and looked around her. "Well, for a start, that couple standing over by that ugly stone angel are Jerrell Bakhash and his wife, Sharifa. He's Lebanese and I think she's Egyptian. Funny mix, eh?"

"Well, it's the same part of the world, I guess. What line of business is he in?"

"He's got some kind of ready-made garment factory. The couple next to them own an Italian restaurant . . . Romeo's Palace or something like that . . . and his name is Dario Grosso, and that's his wife, Hadeya, next to him. She's Sharifa Bakhash's sister." She stopped and gave a slight nod toward the open grave. "You said that Arnold Schaefer gave you this list, so you already know him, and that's Thelma, his wife, in the wheelchair next to Jacquelyn Dubois."

"Do you know Maurice's former wives?"

"Not really. I heard that Maurice and Annette were very young when they were married and they broke up soon after moving to Vancouver."

"What about his second wife?"

"Edith? He was married to her for quite a long time—maybe fifteen years. Then, of course, Jacquelyn happened." She stopped talking as her husband started toward them, and she thrust the list back into Maggie's hands. "Here, you'd better take this."

"Would you please call me?" Maggie said as she quickly pushed one of the agency's cards into Stella's hands. "You've been such a help."

"Come along, Stella." Robert Edgeworthy took his wife firmly by the elbow and hurried her down the path.

"Who's the woman you were talking to?" Nat asked as they walked toward their car.

"Stella Edgeworthy, and she and her husband were on that fishing trip. She gave me quite a bit of information on the other guests, too," she added as she got into the passenger seat. "Then her husband turned up and hustled her off. I've asked her to call me but I don't expect she will. Why's George here?" she asked as she stowed her handbag on the floor. "Don't tell me he's working on this case, too?"

"Not exactly. The West Van cops have the murder in hand, but George says the Vancouver police have an interest in the late Maurice and his friends."

"That's going to make things interesting."

"You can say that again," Nat said grimly. "Especially if Inspector Mark Farthing gets a whiff we're on the case, too." Nat and the inspector didn't exactly see eye to eye. When Nat retired from the Vancouver police force, Farthing had taken over his old job. Since that time, the man had been promoted several ranks and really felt his position.

TO MAGGIE'S SURPRISE, STELLA Edgeworthy did phone just after ten the next morning. "Robert said I should call you."

"That's great!" Maggie said, but she was a little puzzled. Stella's husband hadn't appeared too happy to see them talking together. "You could be a great help in the investigation. After all, you were probably one of the last people to see Maurice alive."

"I suppose so," Stella answered. "If you really think I could help . . ."

"What about two this afternoon?" Maggie said. "You have our address?"

"Two's fine."

"I'VE NEVER BEEN IN a private detective's office before," Stella said after Maggie had settled her in the visitor's chair. She had discarded the sombre clothes from the day of the funeral and was now wearing a leaf-green wool dress and matching coat that accentuated her curly auburn hair and hazel eyes. "Whatever made you take up a job like this?"

"Long story," Maggie replied, smiling. "Now, while we're waiting for Henny to bring in some coffee, what about taking another look at these names and telling me if anyone is missing?"

"For a start," Stella replied, taking the sheet of paper from Maggie, "there are only six names here." She laughed nervously. "Of course, Schaefer gave you this, so he wouldn't count the women."

"I've already found that out," Maggie said, handing her a pen. "So how about completing the list for me?"

"I see you've filled in the ones I gave you yesterday." She opened her large handbag and dived down into its depths. Maggie's heart sank as she watched Stella pull out a crumpled pack of Lucky Strikes and a lighter. "You don't mind, do you?" she asked, lighting up before looking down at the list again. "Do you have an ashtray?"

"I don't smoke," Maggie said pointedly, "but I'll try and find you one." She pressed the intercom button, hoping that Henny wouldn't panic.

It took a few minutes, but eventually Henny's voice boomed, "What you want, Mrs. Maggie?"

"Have we any ashtrays?"

"Why? Only Mr. Nat smoke."

"My client needs one."

"Oh!" Maggie could hear the disapproval. "I find something."

"And Henry Smith's wife is Rosie. They come from London—Cockneys, I think they're called—and she wears the most godawful clothes you've ever seen. Absolutely no taste whatever." She flicked her ash onto the carpet just as Henny walked in carrying a tray with two cups of coffee and an extra white china saucer.

"Here," Henny said pointedly, placing the saucer next to Stella. "For ash. And here is coffee."

"Uh . . . thanks." Stella glanced back at the list. "Where was I?"

"You were describing Rosie Smith."

"They own the Exotic Eastern Emporium on Pender." Stella gave a derisive laugh. "It's sort of an antique store. And their two sons were there, Job and Noah. A couple of thugs, if you ask me." She took a drag before carrying on. "And the last name on the list is Liam Mahaffy. He's not married and he's into horses. You know," she added seeing the confused look on Maggie's face, "race horses. Has a stud farm out in Delta. Oodles of money. And he's quite a dish."

"So that makes nine men and five women."

"No, just four women. Thelma Schaefer never comes to things like that," she answered as she crushed out the cigarette. "And it only adds up to nine men if you count Maurice."

"Had you met any of them before?"

"Yeah, Maurice had us all come to an *informative lunch*, as he called it." When Maggie looked puzzled, Stella continued, "You know the kind of thing—overcooked chicken and soggy rice and peas, projector with slides of the area, artist's impression of how it will look when completed . . ."

"You knew Maurice and his wife socially, I take it?"

She shook her head. "Robert knew him through business deals."

"What kind of deals?"

Stella shrugged. "Robert never brings his business home," she said evasively.

"Were both the Schaefers at that lunch?"

"Just Arnold. He was very loud and sceptical. Thelma's a real saint to put up with him."

"Do you know if any of the women have careers?"

"Rosie helps her husband run the Emporium. I don't know about the Egyptian sisters."

"What does your husband do?"

"Real estate."

"He sells houses?"

"God, no," she answered disparagingly. "Big land deals, businesses, that sort of thing."

Maggie reached across the desk for the list. "So was your husband in on these deals with Dubois?"

She shrugged. "As I said, he doesn't bring business home."

"Schaefer intimated that Maurice had a roving eye." Maggie said.

"Well, yes, he liked to flirt. No real harm in it."

"Did you see him leave the lodge that Saturday?"

"No. But I saw him down on the dock just before lunch. I thought it was odd because I assumed he'd gone fishing with the others, then I got talking to Rosie Smith—she was ranting on about her miserable grandchildren—and I forgot all about it."

"Did you tell the police you'd seen him on the dock?" Maggie asked, taking a sip of her coffee.

Stella shook her head. "They didn't ask me." She reached into her handbag for another cigarette and Maggie noticed the slight tremble in her hands as she opened the pack.

"So when did you know that he was missing?"

"When he didn't turn up for dinner that night at the lodge. Arnold went over to his cabin, but there was no sign of him or his gear."

"Did the lodge organize a search party?"

"It was too dark, so we had to wait until morning, then we split up and searched the trails and along the beach. I don't think anyone looked too hard, because all his stuff was gone from his cabin, you see, so we figured he'd got a lift back to Vancouver."

Maggie looked up as Nat walked quietly into the room. "Stella, I'd like you to meet my partner, Nat Southby. We're just about finished," Maggie told him. "Just one more question, Stella. You said you thought he might have got a lift back to the city. Were there other guests at the lodge outside of your party?"

Stella began digging in her bag for her lighter. "No. Well, yes, I guess there might have been, but they didn't come into the lodge for meals." Maggie noticed that her hands were shaking quite badly as she lit her cigarette.

"WAS SHE ANY HELP?" Nat asked, when Maggie returned from seeing Stella out.

Maggie nodded before walking over to the window and throwing it open to clear the smoke. "A regular little goldmine. Sit down and tell me, what's odd about this list?"

She had barely finished reading out the list of people who had been at the lodge when Nat said, "They have nothing in common—different nationalities, different occupations, different social classes . . ."

"And there's something else, Nat. That woman knows something that she doesn't want to tell me."

IT WAS AROUND EIGHT o'clock that evening and Maggie had just relaxed by her fireplace when the telephone rang. It was Harry.

"Margaret, I've been worrying about that house you inherited in Quebec."

"But . . ."

"Just hear me out. I've just heard on the radio that the weather is at its worst back there and you have left the house empty, and you know you can't rely on neighbours. I've talked to a lawyer friend of mine in Montreal, and he's agreed to look after all the arrangements of putting it on the market."

"Harry, calm down," she said when he finally paused for breath. "I have rented it to an aircraft engineer and his wife. They're from England, and he's just started working at an aircraft factory in Montreal. Apparently, they are thrilled to bits with the house."

"Oh, I see. Well, I was only thinking of your interests, Margaret. I still think you should sell it."

"I probably will one day. Now, how are you, Harry?" She wished she hadn't asked that question when he began to tell her.

## CHAPTER FOUR

Maggie had been wakened several times during the night by the branches on the big old maple tree banging against her bedroom window. Tired and bad-tempered, she groggily made breakfast for herself and the two animals.

"I don't suppose you'd use the back garden?" Maggie asked the dog, who was waiting patiently at her feet with his lead in his mouth. Oscar, reared in the cold winters of Quebec, just thumped his tail and headed for the front door. Emily, looking disdainfully at both Maggie and Oscar, curled herself into a tight ball and went back to sleep in her basket.

The walk in the wet and windy morning did them both good, and Maggie was in a better frame of mind when she let the dog back inside the house. "That will have to do you until Carole comes," she said as she removed his leash. Carole, a teenaged neighbour, loved Oscar and willingly took him for a walk after school each day.

After making sure the door was firmly locked, Maggie walked down the long back garden to the garage where she kept her car, her mind already on the day ahead.

As usual, Henny was in the office before Maggie and Nat. A sombre grey suit and matching grey lisle stockings had replaced her usual brown serge. The only concession to contrast was a mustard yellow hand-knitted sweater, but her shoes were still her everyday no-nonsense brown oxfords.

"Your face all rosy," she greeted Maggie.

"I had a long walk with Oscar," she answered.

"Mr. Nat's old wife called already."

"And what did Nancy want?"

"She said to tell him she is coming in to see him about ten o'clock."

"That's all we need."

"HOW ARE WE GOING to split these interviews up?" Maggie asked. They were seated in her office, going over the list of names.

"Why don't you tackle Jerrell Bakhash and I'll visit Romeo's Palace? And although you've interviewed Stella Edgeworthy, I'd like to have a chat with her husband."

"The real estate angle, you mean?"

"Yeah."

"That's a good idea," Maggie answered. "Although Stella did give us a good description of the guests staying at the lodge, her husband's view could be quite different. Oh, and by the way, did Henny tell you that Nancy's coming in this morning?"

"Yeah," he grimaced. "Can't think what she wants this time."

"I SAW YOU AT the funeral last Thursday," Nancy hip-checked Nat's door closed and flung her imitation leopard skin coat over the back of a chair. "I suppose it was too much for you to speak to me?"

"Didn't see you, Nancy. What do you want?"

"I want to know how the investigation is going."

"Why do you need to know?"

"I invested in Maurice's ski resort."

"What ski resort?"

"It's on Hollyburn."

"That big clear-cut on the north side?"

"How should I know? I don't ski."

"Where did you get the money to invest?"

"None of your business," she said defiantly.

Nat shrugged. "What about the Pender Harbour deal? Did you get involved in that scheme, too?"

Nancy laughed. "You have to have real money for that one. He was asking thirty thousand a share."

"Well, if you're so worried about your investment, go and see your friend Jacquelyn."

"She's not a friend, Nat. After all, the girl's only in her early twenties and she hadn't a clue what her husband was up to. She's only interested in getting Maurice's will settled, because she's running out of money. I don't know why she doesn't sell some of that stuff that Maurice collected—there's a whole bunch of these old Egyptian cats and statues and bowls and old jewellery and stuff like that."

"Have you seen this stuff, as you call it?"

"Yeah. When I was over at her house a few weeks back."

"How did you meet her, anyway?"

"It was at that presentation lunch for Secret Valley—that's the ski resort. She was acting hostess for her husband and his partner."

"Partner? Who's the partner?"

"Can't remember his name. Anyway, he didn't turn up. But I guess Jacquelyn gets half the ski resort, too."

"She didn't do so badly for a six-month marriage," Nat commented, grinning.

"Yeah!" Nancy answered as she pulled her fur coat on. "She's done okay for herself." Then she added venomously, "Considering she was some kinda dancer when Maurice met her."

"Oh?" he asked, raising an eyebrow.

"Yeah. Anyhow, she won't get much out of it if his two ex-wives have their way. They're going to contest the will on behalf of his son and daughter." And she sailed out the door.

"How about that?" Maggie exclaimed later when Nat had filled her in on Nancy's visit. "That means that we found Dubois's body right next to his own clear-cut."

"That's something we've got to look into. And we need to know how he found his prospective investors." He paused for a moment. "When are you going to see Jerrell Bakhash?"

"Tomorrow. I've got a ten o'clock appointment. Isn't that the same time you're seeing Robert Edgeworthy?"

"Ten-thirty, and then I'll drive back to town for my interview with the Grossos."

MAGGIE CLIMBED OUT OF her car and approached the front entrance of Jerrell Bakhash and Son. The business was located in the dingiest part of Powell Street. The scarred wooden building with its filthy iron-grilled windows sent a shudder down her spine. She couldn't imagine why anyone would want to work in such an environment. The faded wooden sign nailed to the scuffed front door stated that they manufactured garments for the whole family.

There was no one attending the reception desk. After calling out several times, she realized that no one would hear her anyway over the volume of noise coming from behind two swinging doors. Pushing them open, she found herself in an enormous room, and the noise, she realized, was coming from the row upon row of industrial sewing machines manned by women of all nationalities. A sea of faces glanced up momentarily at her before bending again over their machines. She stood there for quite a few minutes before a woman in the front row yelled at her over the noise.

"There's no work. All machines taken."

"I'm here to see Mr. Bakhash."

"Upstairs in his office. Outside." She turned her attention back to her machine.

Feeling suitably dismissed, Maggie went back into the deserted reception area. *Outside! Did she mean outside the building?* Then she saw a narrow uncarpeted staircase to the right of the entranceway and a small sign pointing upward. *Office and Cutting Rooms.*

The door at the top of the stairs opened onto a narrow walkway, offices and rooms on one side and a waist-high partition on the other that gave a full view of the dusty sewing room down below. Looking over the railing, Maggie could see that there was hardly any room to move between the sewing machine tables, and she wondered how the women could possibly breathe in the lint-filled air. Mr. Bakhash's office, a large glass-fronted room, was halfway down the walkway. She tapped on the door and pushed it open.

"Can I help you?" asked the secretary, a smartly dressed blonde, probably in her early thirties.

"Mrs. Spencer. I called yesterday."

"He's expecting you. Go straight in."

Maggie's feet sank into plush carpet as she walked toward the tall man standing behind a desk piled high with swatches of material. Dark brown hair, brown eyes peering at her through horn-rimmed glasses, he was dressed in a well-cut heather tweed suit. He leaned over the desk to shake hands before indicating for her to sit in one of the visitors' chairs. He took a sip from a small cup containing thick Turkish coffee before he turned to Maggie. "Now what's this about?"

"It's about Mr. Dubois," Maggie answered, handing one of her business cards to him. "Our firm has been retained to look into his death."

"But I hardly knew the man." Although Bakhash had a strong Middle Eastern accent, his English was perfect.

"But you and your wife were with him at the fishing lodge over New Year's."

"That was business."

"You were planning to invest in the St. Clare Cove properties?"

"You know about that? But what has that to do with Dubois's death?"

"We're not sure, Mr. Bakhash. Would you mind telling me how you got on to this venture?" She glanced up at the secretary and mouthed a "thank you" as the girl placed a china cup and saucer at her elbow.

Jerrell Bakhash leaned back into his leather chair, took a puff on his fat cigar and then a sip of coffee before answering. "It was an ad in the *Sun* newspaper," he said, riffling through the contents of the wallet he'd taken from an inner pocket of his jacket. "I thought I had kept it, but I guess I must've thrown it out. Anyway, it said in essence that an invitation was extended to discriminating investors interested in an 'unusual business adventure.' So I answered it and the upshot was an invitation to this lodge—meals and accommodation included." Then he added with a sly grin, "Who's going to turn down an offer like that?"

"And did you?"

"Did I what?" He looked puzzled for a moment before leaning toward her. "Oh, you mean did I invest? It has its possibilities, but . . ." Slowly he shook his head. "The area is very, very beautiful but it is also very remote."

"But there is a road all the way to Pender Harbour, isn't there?"

He nodded in agreement. "But imagine anyone slightly interested in the project who has already been on a ferry that has taken forever to cross from Horseshoe Bay to Gibsons Landing, driven over ten miles to get to Sechelt and then has to face at least another ten miles of a road that twists and turns like a drunken snake." He paused. "Have you been there?"

"Once. But I was a guest offshore, on one of the islands," Maggie answered, recalling her imprisonment and escape from the island on her very first case with Nat. "But I have to agree with you, it is very beautiful and there must be a lot of people looking for that that kind of tranquility."

He nodded. "You may be right. Now what did you want to know?"

"Exactly what was Mr. Dubois offering his prospective customers?"

"I think he bought the place figuring he would make money on it as a resort, but it is very old and rundown and it would take a helluva lot of money to fix it up." He gave a laugh. "So the only way Maurice was going to get his investment back was to parcel it up in lots and sell them."

"Were you out fishing with the others the day that Dubois took off?"

"In a manner of speaking," he answered. "There were so many of us that we had to take three boats out. I was with a young man named Noah Smith. Didn't stay out long. Man's a complete bore and the fish weren't biting."

"Was Dubois there when you got back?"

He shrugged. "Didn't notice. My wife was playing bridge or something, so I went back to our cabin to sleep."

"Do you think I could talk to your wife?"

"What's the point? She's talked to the police and told them she didn't see Dubois take off."

"I'll only contact her if I think it's necessary, okay?"

He shrugged. "Phone her first. Miss Willis will give you the number."

"Thanks for letting me take up your time," Maggie said, rising from her chair.

"How'd you like a look around?" he asked, opening the door for her. "Come along. I'll show you the cutting room."

"Thanks. I'd like that," she answered. "I've always wanted to know how ready-made garments were cut out."

"It's the same as when you sew at home," he replied, "but on a much bigger scale, as several garments are cut at the same time."

"By hand?" Maggie asked.

"No, no!" he laughed. "A cutting machine. Like a big cookie cutter."

Moments later she was in the long cutting room and watching as two men skilfully guided the huge cutting knives through several layers of material around thick cardboard patterns.

"Men's shirts," Bakhash said. "Our most popular brand."

"Then what happens to them?" Maggie asked, fascinated.

"The pieces go down to the sewing floor below to be sewn up by the girls." He led the way out of the room and, leaning over the low railing, pointed down to where the women sat at their machines.

"They must be very skilled."

Bakhash laughed as he pulled himself away from the railing. "Most of 'em just sew straight seams. Only the more experienced women sew the tricky bits." He led the way back to his office and opened the door. "Miss Willis, give this lady my address and phone number." He turned back to Maggie. "Best of luck on your investigation. You can see yourself out?"

Maggie sat in her car for a few minutes writing up her notes on the interview. "That was all very interesting," she said as she snapped her steno pad shut and stowed it into her bag, "but I don't think I'm any further ahead."

She pushed the car into gear but had to wait a few moments until an old army Jeep clattered past her and parked near the rear entrance of Bakhash and Son. She watched idly as a young man jumped out of it and dashed into the building. He looked vaguely familiar, but so many young men looked alike these days. *Perhaps he's the "and son,"* she thought. It wasn't until she was driving back to the office that it occurred to her that the young man had actually looked very much like Maurice Dubois's son.

MEANWHILE, NAT HAD DRIVEN along East Hastings, found the Edgeworthy Real Estate office and managed to park in a spot right outside the building.

"Can I be of assistance?" The young redheaded receptionist beamed her professional smile at him. The wooden nameplate announced she was Miss Eileen Murphy.

"Nat Southby to see Mr. Edgeworthy."

She glanced down at her appointment book. "He'll be with you shortly. Please have a seat. Coffee?"

Nat shook his head and, sitting in one of the padded chairs, surveyed the office. Miss Murphy sat behind a low counter. On the wall behind her were numerous photographs of office buildings, waterfront acreages, estate type houses, stores and factories.

"Mr. Edgeworthy doesn't deal in ordinary housing?" he asked.

"No. Mostly businesses."

Nat walked closer to the wall. "What about this place?" he asked, indicating an artist's impression of a large log structure, interior designs, ski runs and chairlifts.

"Secret Valley. Looks wonderful, doesn't it? That's one of Mr. Edgeworthy's newest projects. A great investment opportunity."

Suddenly, one of the two inner doors opened and Robert Edgeworthy emerged with a man wearing an overcoat and carrying a briefcase. "You won't regret making this investment,

Mr. Blythe," he said as he escorted the man to the door. Then, as he walked back to his office, he nodded to Nat. "You wanted to see me?"

Nat nodded and followed Edgeworthy in. "You were a friend of Maurice Dubois?" he asked, passing his business card over.

"Business acquaintance. Didn't know the man socially."

"What about the St. Clare deal?"

"That old fishing camp? Dubois had approached me on it, and to be perfectly frank, it was one of the reasons the wife and I were up there at New Year's." He laughed. "You know the old saying, 'don't buy a pig in a poke.'"

"Is it a good deal?"

"Beautiful spot, waterfront property, perfect view lots. Dubois had quite a good concept, really, but I don't think it's the right time."

"Too remote?"

Edgeworthy nodded. "That and the problem of commuting. Give the Sunshine Coast another twenty-five years and maybe it will really come into its own, and then condominiums and town-houses will go over in a big way."

"Then it wouldn't be a good thing to invest in now?" Nat asked.

"Big risk. As I say, maybe twenty-five years from now. But I'm sure you're not here to talk about real estate."

"You're right. Any ideas why Dubois was killed?"

Edgeworthy shook his head. "I can't say I liked the guy that much, but I have no idea why anyone would want to murder him."

Nat took him step by step through his New Year's stay at the lodge, but the conclusion was that Edgeworthy, like the others, had thought that Dubois was out fishing that Saturday afternoon in one of the other boats, and he said he was completely mystified how the man's body could have ended up on Hollyburn Mountain.

"What happens to the St. Clare Cove property now?" Nat asked as he prepared to leave.

"Dubois had only put a down payment on it so it, will go back to the original owner," he answered. "Unless, of course, his widow is prepared to take on the debt."

Nat couldn't see Jacquelyn footing that bill, and he got up to leave. He turned just before opening the door. "I was admiring the drawings of another project you're interested in. Your receptionist said it's called Secret Valley. What's that all about?"

"Are you into skiing? If so, that's going to be a really great deal. Ski lodge, saunas, indoor pool, massage—all that kind of thing."

"I've never heard of Secret Valley. Where's it located?"

"Hollyburn Mountain. That area is going to boom, and if you're interested, the receptionist will give you a brochure."

"Thanks. I'll pick one up on my way out."

NAT FOUND ROMEO'S PALACE quite easily. The Italian restaurant had booths upholstered in red plush along two walls, and round tables covered in white tablecloths in the main part of the restaurant, each table adorned with a red candle stuck into a basket-covered Chianti bottle. A well-stocked bar was located across the back wall. Hadeya and Dario were a sharp contrast: Hadeya was a classic Egyptian beauty—olive skin, dark hair and a voluptuous body—while Dario was a handsome, swarthy-skinned, brown-eyed Italian of medium height. Hadeya's older sister, Sharifa, they told Nat, had persuaded them to go to the resort over New Year's and they had shared a large cabin with the Bakhashes.

"Which part of Italy did you come from?" Nat asked over a cup of coffee.

"Oh, I'm third generation Canadian," he answered. "My grandparents emigrated to Montreal in the early 1900s. And I met Hadeya in Montreal when she came to visit her sister after the war."

Nat nodded before asking if either of them had seen Maurice on that particular Saturday afternoon. But Dario said he had gone fishing with that strange Englishman Smith, and his wife had been with the other women in the lodge.

MAGGIE AND NAT ARRIVED back at the office within a half hour of each other.

"So how was lunch?" Maggie asked, taking a bite of the sandwich she had brought from home. "Did George enlighten you?" George had called Nat the previous day to arrange one of their regular lunch get-togethers. "You never know," he had said to Maggie before she had left for her interview with Bakhash. "George might let something slip on why he was at the Dubois funeral."

"No. He asked a few questions about the other guests at the resort. But as I told him, we've only just started to interview them ourselves. So tell me about Bakhash?"

"He has an accent, but his English is impeccable. I would say he's the product of an expensive English boarding school of some sort. But that factory is something else . . ." And she proceeded to fill Nat in on the interview and her visit to the cutting room.

"Can't imagine anyone working in those conditions," Nat commented after she told him about the row upon row of sewing machines.

"I would think a lot of those women are immigrants with very little English," Maggie said sadly, "and they can't get any other kind of job."

Nat filled her in on his brief visit with Robert Edgeworthy. "So apparently no one at the fishing resort actually saw Maurice

Dubois leave." He paused for a moment. "But I did learn some more about that ski resort investment of Nancy's." He threw the brochure over to her. "Take a look at that."

Maggie looked up from reading the brochure. "A fifteen hundred dollar deposit! Does Nancy have that kind of money?"

"No," he answered grimly. "What's next on the agenda?"

"You're off the hook tomorrow, but I'm seeing Henry and Rosie Smith around ten. And I've arranged for us to see Liam Mahaffy at his stud farm in Delta on Saturday. Oh, that must be Henny," she added, hearing the outer door open.

"Did you get message?" Henny asked, poking her head into Maggie's office.

"No."

"It is on your desk." She rummaged among the papers on Maggie's desk until she came up with a torn-off scrap, which she handed to Maggie. "It's that funny French lady. She called and said it is urgent for you or Mr. Nat to call her back."

"Did she say what it was all about?"

"No. She just say it is very urgent. I tell her that you and Mr. Nat are out on business, like you tell me to say," she said disapprovingly.

Maggie hid a smile as she reached for the telephone.

"Somebody has robbed my house," Jacquelyn said when she answered the phone.

"Have you called the police?"

"*Non, non!* I have already told you I cannot do that. You must come!"

Maggie glanced at the wall clock. "We'll be with you about two-thirty, okay?"

After she hung up, Maggie told Nat, "I think I'll order some telephone notepads for Henny. What do you think?"

Nat grinned. "Might not be a bad idea."

THE DUBOIS ADDRESS WAS rather impressive. It was a large red brick house behind wrought-iron railings and gates on Southwest Marine Drive. Maggie realized that it was not far from the home of her elder daughter—but Barbara's house was just half the size of Jacquelyn's.

A woman in a black dress and apron let them in and showed them into a living room where antique tables jostled for place with two red velour chesterfields and two armchairs, a cretonne-covered wingback on one side of the fireplace and a matching love seat on the other. "Mrs. Dubois will be with you in a moment."

"Would you take a look at this place?" Nat whispered as he sat gingerly on the very edge of the wingback's seat cushion.

"I see you have come." A pale-faced Jacquelyn with dark rings under her eyes walked into the room and stood in front of Nat. He immediately got to his feet.

"You must call the Vancouver police," he told her.

She shook her head. "My Maurice say," Jacquelyn said tearfully, "that the police are good for nothing. And the antiquities are a secret between him and me."

"Antiquities?" Nat asked, looking around the still very full living room.

"Egyptian antiquities. They take all the pieces that Maurice find in Egypt. Look, I show you." She led them through to the library and pointed to a photo album lying open on a Duncan Fyffe table. "See? My Maurice always keep the pictures."

The album contained page after page of photos of gold masks, bowls that looked as if it they were made of beaten gold, a half dozen cups and vases, small gem-studded figurines and a black cat that appeared to have been carved from ebony. There was jewellery as well—bracelets, earrings, bangles, rings, combs and even a couple of tiaras—and they all appeared to be made of chased silver, turquoise and other precious stones. Another picture showed several small carved stones.

"These look very old," Maggie whispered, awed. "Are they for real?"

"My Maurice would never have imitations."

"You mean they came out of Egyptian tombs?" Maggie asked.

"My husband is not a grave robber," Jacquelyn answered haughtily.

"But where did he get this stuff?" Nat asked.

She shrugged. "It was before I met him."

"What about insurance?" Maggie asked.

"No insurance. Some he kept always locked in the safe but most was in his den. Come."

The den was at the back of the house, and Maggie immediately walked over to the French doors that opened onto a red and grey brick patio with a stone balustrade. Beyond it, steps led down to a lush lawn and flowerbeds. "Is this where they broke in?"

Jacquelyn nodded.

Maggie examined the doors closely, but the lock had not been forced and there was no broken glass on the floor. She pointed this out to Nat and then asked Jacquelyn, "Do any of your late husband's family own keys to your house?"

Jacquelyn shook her head. "The real estate office changed all the locks when Maurice buy the house for me."

"Which real estate company?"

Jacquelyn shrugged and raised her manicured hands skyward.

"The thieves must have got a key from someone," Maggie argued.

"It is a great mystery," Jacquelyn Dubois answered.

"Is this where the stuff was displayed?" Nat asked, pointing to three tall cabinets. Each had solid oak doors that covered inner glass doors, but both sets of doors were now wide open and the shelves were bare.

"*Oui.*" Jacquelyn dabbed at her swollen eyes. "*Mes précieux bijoux.*"

"What about the safe?"

"That is empty, too, see?"

Nat peered into the wall safe. "You've got to call the police, Mrs. Dubois. You need to show those pictures to them."

"*Non, non!* I tell you Maurice was ... what you say ... very strong that I am never to tell police. But you must get them back for me."

"Are you sure the safe was locked?" Maggie asked.

"And when was the last time you opened it?" Nat added.

Jacquelyn Dubois looked away for a moment. "Yesterday. I take out some cash," she replied and then shrugged. "I am sure I locked it."

"And nothing else was taken?"

"Already I tell you," she answered angrily. "*Rien.*"

"Do you have any idea who the thieves were? It's obvious that they knew exactly what was in those cupboards and in that safe."

"But nobody know about Maurice's *objets!* The doors are always closed. See, like this!" And she demonstrated how the double set of doors closed and locked. "And Maurice say it is our secret."

"Did you ever wear any of that jewellery?" Nat asked.

"Only once. Maurice let me wear the bracelet with the blue beads to a big party. But it is too heavy and Maurice worry all the time that I lose it."

"Did your maid hear anything?" Maggie asked.

"My maid? Oh, you mean Theresa, my cleaning woman. She doesn't come in until nine in the morning."

"You'd better show us the rest of the house," Nat said, walking toward the door. But it was just as Jacquelyn had said—nothing else had been disturbed.

"THE THIEVES KNEW EXACTLY what they wanted," Nat said on their way back to the office. "And that was the Egyptian antiquities."

"Yes," Maggie answered. "But the widow's hands are still loaded with rings and they must be worth a mint!"

THE EXOTIC EASTERN EMPORIUM was a bit of a shock to Maggie's rather conservative taste. As she stepped into the old building, she found herself overwhelmed by the heavy smell of incense, dust and old carpets. She wended her way carefully between tall Chinese vases, tables laden with Indian brassware, smiling Buddhas, scarabs of all sizes and mixed authenticity, decorative inlaid mahogany chests and black lacquered tables. Masses of carpets of varying sizes were piled on the floor or hanging on the walls. At the back of the store, a thin, henna-dyed woman was busy wrapping one of the Indian brass vases in a sheet of newspaper before slipping it into a paper bag.

"There you are then, luv," she said to her customer. "Don't use brass polish on it. Just give it a quick rub up with a duster." As she handed the man his change, her bright button eyes took in Maggie.

"So what can I do for you, dear?" Her London accent sounded as if she had only just got off the boat.

"I'm Maggie Spencer. I called yesterday?"

"Oh, that detective agency lady. I'm Rosie Smith. Just wait a sec while I get my youngest out here. "Noah!" she yelled. "Come out and mind the shop."

A hulking thirty-year-old appeared from somewhere, and a

few moments later Maggie found herself in a back room, seated at a wooden table with a stewed cup of tea and a digestive biscuit in front of her.

"You this detective bloke's secretary, then?" a man's enormous voice demanded.

Startled, Maggie turned to see a huge, moustached man glaring down at her. "Partner," she answered, taking a sip of the bitter brew.

"This my tea, Rosie?" he asked, dropping four sugar lumps into a cup without waiting for an answer.

"This is my Henry," Rosie said, sitting down opposite Maggie. "Now what do you want to know?"

It took a few seconds for Maggie to pull herself together, as Henry was still standing over her, slurping his tea and chomping on biscuits. "Did you know Maurice Dubois well?"

"Not really, I . . ."

"Didn't know the bloke at all," Henry interrupted his wife.

"We met him up at that fishing camp," Rosie carried on. "Thought it might be a nice place to retire to, but it's too far for our lads to come and visit."

"The only good thing about it," Henry cut in again, "is that it would'a been too far for them to drop their offspring onto us. We done our bit."

"I understand your two sons were at the resort with you."

"Who told you that?" Rosie asked.

"We have a list of people who were there," Maggie answered.

Rosie hesitated for a moment. "Well . . . they wanted to make sure we didn't get taken in." She laughed. "You hear about these confidence tricksters all the time, you know."

"Did you go out fishing?" Maggie asked, turning to Henry Smith.

"Yeah! We caught a salmon."

"And my Henry don't even eat fish!" Rosie said.

"I told Rosie she should've come out with us."

"Didn't have much chance, did I? That Schaefer bloke made it plain that us wives wasn't invited. So I got stuck with that awful Edgeworthy woman yapping at me about her fancy house and her fancy clothes."

"How did you find out about St. Clare Cove?" Maggie asked, trying not to smile.

"Some ad in the newspaper." The sound of a truck pulling up outside made him swallow the rest of his tea in one gulp. "That's the delivery."

"Before you go, Mr. Smith, did you see Maurice Dubois leave the resort?"

"No. It must've been when we was out fishing." Shrugging into a thick mackinaw, he walked toward the back door.

"You've quite a place here," Maggie said as she followed Rosie back to the showroom. "Do you live on the premises?"

"Upstairs. Have a very nice flat up there. You should come back and have a good browse—we've got some very nice genuine Persian rugs."

"I'll keep that in mind," Maggie answered. "Thanks for seeing me."

MAGGIE'S INTERVIEW WITH THE Smiths had only taken a half hour, so on the spur of the moment and after a fast phone call, she was on her way for a quick visit to Jacquelyn Dubois. She needed to get a feel for her lifestyle, her surroundings and more importantly, how the young woman really ticked.

As Maggie walked up the stone-flagged path, she noticed that one of the two garage doors was open and a gleaming white sports car was waiting inside it. The same maid showed her into the living room and told her that Madame Dubois would be with her in a moment. While waiting, Maggie scanned the photographs that were set on the grand piano. Most were of Jacquelyn and Maurice, but a few were of family groups—obviously her parents with a very young Jacquelyn and a couple of siblings. One was of Maurice with his son and daughter, and another showed him in army uniform. Turning from the photographs, she re-examined the beautiful room.

"Ah, Mrs. Spencer, how nice to see you," Jacquelyn said, coming into the room and extending her hand. "You are making progress, *oui*? You have find my Maurice's antiquities?"

"Not yet. We're still interviewing the people who were at the fishing lodge. In fact, I have just left Henry and Rosie Smith's emporium. Quite a place! Have you been there?"

"My Maurice take me a few times to pick up or buy something, I can't think what. It is a very cheap place. Full of—what do you call it—junk?"

"I have a list of the lodge's guests here," Maggie said, taking it from her handbag. "Do you recognize any of the names?"

Jacquelyn barely glanced at the paper before handing it back. "I know Arnold Schaefer, but the others I do not know. Now, if there is nothing else, I have a lunch engagement."

Maggie started toward the door but turned suddenly. "Your husband was in the army?" She waved a hand toward the picture on the grand piano.

Her face brightened. "Ah, yes. The famous Vandoos. He was very proud."

"Just one more thing, Mrs. Dubois—do you know where your stepson works?"

"You mean René? Somewhere in the city. Why?"

"I thought I saw him the other day at a garment factory run by Jerrell Bakhash."

"Who is this Bakhash person?"

"He and his wife were at the fishing lodge."

"You must be mistaken. It could not be René at a garment factory. Now if you excuse me."

As Maggie left the house, she glanced toward the garage again. Jacquelyn was already climbing into the white sports car. *I guess she really is going out.*

## CHAPTER FIVE

Barbara was surprised to see her mother at the front door. "What's wrong?" There was no "how are you" or "it's so nice to see you, Mom."

"I was visiting a client close by so I thought I'd call in to see how you are." Maggie followed her elder daughter into the large, sunny kitchen at the rear of the house. "It's been quite a while."

"That's not my fault, Mother. You're always so busy at that ridiculous job of yours. Have you spoken to Dad recently?"

"A couple of days ago. Where's Oliver?" Maggie's three-year-old grandson was a source of joy to her, and she was still amazed that Barbara could have produced such a happy and contented baby.

"He's napping. I suppose you're too busy to stay for lunch?"

"I would love to stay for lunch," Maggie answered. "Is it okay if I go up and get Oliver?" Maggie was determined that she was not going to react to the usual unpleasantness about her job or leaving Harry, dating her boss, and most of all, downgrading from the large Kerrisdale house she had shared with Harry to her small one-person house in Kitsilano. It was hard to skirt around these subjects, but Oliver was so demanding of Maggie's attention that the next couple of hours went by very happily.

"THOUGHT YOU'D GOT LOST," Nat greeted her later that afternoon. "Interview took longer than you thought?"

"No. I went to see Jacquelyn after I met with the Smiths, which I will tell you about in a moment. Then since Barbara lives so close to the Dubois house, I decided to pop in and see her."

"How did that go?"

"Very well. She's much . . . I'm not sure how to put it . . . softer since she's had Oliver."

"That's what motherhood does for you," Nat replied with a grin.

"What would you know about that?"

"Not much, I guess, but I often wonder if things would've been different if Nancy and I'd had kids. Anyway, tell me about the Smiths and our client." He listened and made notes as Maggie filled him in on the interviews.

"That man really gave me a scare, Nat. He's huge and really menacing." She paused for a moment, thinking back. "And something struck me as odd. The Smiths absolutely denied knowing Maurice Dubois before, but when I asked Jacquelyn if she knew the Smiths and their emporium, she said that Maurice had taken her there to 'buy or pick up something.'"

"Did she know what he'd bought?"

Maggie laughed. "Well, I can tell you it couldn't have been any of the Smiths' treasures. I've never seen such junk! And you saw the wonderful antique furniture in Jacquelyn's house. I'll get Henny to type these notes up right away. You know," she added, "we seem to be getting the same answers from everyone, and it makes me wonder if it's worth going all that way to Delta to see that horse breeder. What's the name of the place?"

"Twin Maples Stud Farm. We might as well go, just to make sure we've seen everyone. Besides, it's not so far now that the new tunnel is open under the river."

LIAM MAHAFFY'S ACCENT WAS as Northern Irish as his name. "So what can I do for you?" he asked. Two of the biggest German shepherds that Maggie had ever seen stood beside him, daring Nat and Maggie to enter the office.

"Beautiful animals," she said, putting her hand out so each of them could sniff it. "What are their names?"

"Black and Tan—what else?"

"I have a dog of my own," she said, but didn't add that Oscar was less than half the size and was a complete wimp.

When his dogs finally indicated their approval, Mahaffy ushered Nat and Maggie into his comfortable office, a separate building that stood between the main stable and the garage that housed his silver Jaguar. The warm scent of sweet hay and the sounds of a busy and lucrative business wafted through the partially open window to them as they sipped the coffee he provided.

"You have quite a spread here," Nat said, unbuttoning his jacket. "And you seem to have a lot of horses in those stables." They had been thoroughly impressed with the massive stables as they drove through the farm's gate.

Mahaffy nodded. "I board as well as train horses for the track. But you haven't come here to discuss horses."

"Mrs. Dubois has asked Mrs. Spencer and myself to look into her husband's death," Nat explained as he proffered a business card. "Could you tell us how long you had known him?" Nat leaned forward and accepted the cigarette that Mahaffy offered.

Mahaffy glanced at Nat's business card before answering. "Only just met the man."

"I see you were in the army, Mr. Mahaffy," Maggie said, pointing to a photograph on the wall behind his desk.

"Yeah. Monty's 8th Division." Then he added proudly, "I was a lieutenant in the tank corps at El Alamein." He got up from behind his desk and reached for the photograph of a group of soldiers standing in front of a Sherman tank. "Here's my crew," he said, placing it in front of them. "That's me there."

"You all look so young," Maggie remarked. "Have you kept in touch with any of them?"

"Only Arnold Schaefer. We were two of the lucky ones." He was silent for a moment.

"What rank did Mr. Schaefer have?" Nat asked after a respectful moment.

"He became our CO. Good bloke to have around, I can tell you."

"Did you live here before the war?" Maggie asked.

"No. Schaefer persuaded me to immigrate."

"And you went straight into the horse breeding business?"

"Good Lord, no. I had just enough money to buy a small farm on Lulu Island."

"Oh? Whereabouts?" Nat asked. "I used to live out there."

"Woodhead Road. Do you know the area? It's just off No. 5 Road."

"Not very well. We lived over by Railway and Williams."

"I was no good at farming. Sold the acreage off a few years ago but kept the old house. Nice house, but it needs doing up . . ."

"Going back to Pender Harbour," Nat interrupted, "were you interested in buying one of those lots?"

"I have enough on my plate here. Schaefer invited me up and I needed a break. I was rather interested in Dubois's other venture, though."

"The ski lodge?" Maggie asked.

"You've heard about it?"

"Secret Valley. I hear Dubois staged some kind of an introductory lunch?"

"Yeah! He had a good turnout." He laughed. "Perhaps because

it was free food. I hope Dubois's death doesn't put the kibosh on it, but I expect his partner will carry on."

"And who was his partner?"

He hesitated for a fraction of a minute. "Some guy in real estate, I think." He looked up as a girl in jodhpurs opened the door.

"The vet's here, Liam."

"Sorry, folks, gotta go." He glanced casually at Nat's card as he arose from behind his desk. "And it was Dubois's widow that called you in?" He raised his eyebrows. "Why isn't she letting the police get on with it?"

"She wasn't happy with the way they were handling it," Nat answered, standing up. He reached across the desk and shook Mahaffy's hand. "Thanks for seeing us."

After they left, Mahaffy slowly tapped the card on his teeth and watched the two of them climb into Maggie's red Morris Minor.

"SO WHAT DO YOU think of our Irish boy?" Maggie asked as she swung the car out of the gate. "And did you see that silver Jag in the garage next to his office?"

"I was more interested in the fact that he and Arnold Schaefer were in the army together."

"Yes, isn't that something? I'm glad you didn't tell him that Nancy was at that lunch. I think we should keep that to ourselves for a bit."

"I almost did mention it," he admitted. "I get so steamed up when I think of her investing money she doesn't have."

"It's her money, Nat."

"That's the point. It isn't," he growled.

To change the subject, Maggie said as lightly as she could, "It's such a beautiful day, why don't we have lunch somewhere and then call on Midge and see how she's making out with that puppy of hers?" Maggie knew that her younger daughter, Midge, an operating room nurse at the Royal Columbian Hospital, had Saturday afternoons off, and the puppy she was referring to was Snowball, a beautiful white Sealyham that a grateful client had insisted on giving to Maggie after their last case. But Emily and Oscar had been enough for Maggie to cope with in her small house, and Midge and Snowball were made for each other.

"Great idea," Nat answered. "Let's call Midge and get her to meet us at that new Italian restaurant, Angelo's, I think it was called. You remember? It's just a stone's throw from her place."

Maggie readily agreed and an hour later the three of them were sitting in a booth, sipping red wine and waiting in anticipation for their Pasta Primavera to arrive. The meal was wonderful and the talk just flowed between them as they ate and then had a leisurely coffee.

"Thanks for a lovely lunch," Midge said finally, getting to her feet. "I'd better get home and find out what Snowball has chewed up this time."

Later, when Maggie and Nat arrived at her house, she was very glad that Oscar's puppy days were well behind him. The place was just as she had left it early that morning.

SUNDAY WAS A TYPICAL February day in Vancouver. It had turned from warm and sunny to cold, wet and windy. Maggie had just settled down to a late supper by the fireside when the phone gave an unwelcome ring.

"Damn!" She glanced at her watch; it was eight fifteen. Nat, she knew, was on a stakeout on an arson case, and she'd spoken to both of her daughters that morning. Reluctantly, she reached for the offending instrument.

"Sorry to interrupt your evening, Mrs. Spencer. It's Julie from your answering service. A woman has called twice for

Mr. Southby, but I can't reach him. She insists it's a matter of life or death . . . so I thought I'd better call you."

"Did she give you a name?"

"That's what's odd. She's quite distraught and she seems to be whispering, but I think she said that her name is Southby."

"You'd better patch her through."

"I've been trying to get Nat for hours!" Nancy was whispering, but the urgency in her voice still came through loud and clear. "Is he there with you?"

"No. What's wrong?"

"I'm locked in this office and I can't get out."

"What office?"

"It's a real estate office on Hastings."

"Call the owners."

"They don't know I'm here."

"Then what in God's name are you doing there?" Maggie snapped.

"I came to get my money back."

"What money?" Maggie insisted.

"Oh! For God's sake. The deposit I made on that ski lodge. Just get hold of that husband of mine. He must be able to pick locks or something."

It was on the tip of Maggie's tongue to point out that Nat *wasn't* Nancy's husband and that he was a detective, not a burglar, but she decided this wasn't the time. She debated hanging up on the woman, but decided against that too. "Where are you?"

"Edgeworthy's Real Estate. On East Hastings."

"Where on Hastings?"

"I don't know. It's near the PNE."

"It's going to take me at least a half hour to get there."

"What about Nat?"

"He's away. It's either me or the fire brigade. Take your pick."

When there was no answer, she slammed the receiver down, took a last bite of her now cold beef stew and put the plate on the kitchen floor for Oscar to finish.

The wind and rain tore at her hooded raincoat as she ran down to the end of the garden, scraped open the garage doors and flung herself into her Morris Minor.

"What in hell has that damned woman got herself into now?" She slammed the car into first gear and drove down the alleyway, turned right onto Trimble and then swung onto Fourth. "The things I do for you, Nat!" she muttered. "You definitely owe me for this one!"

The real estate office, when she finally found it, was a two-storey structure between a shoe repair and a used bookstore. Knowing that the car would be very conspicuous if parked out front on a Sunday evening, she turned down Nanaimo and then drove along the alleyway until she located the back of the office. The three businesses shared a small, muddy parking lot, and except for a tiny glimmer of light from somewhere deep within the bookstore, all of them were in total darkness.

The wind whipped the hood from her head and the icy rain lashed her face as she stepped out of the car to make her way to the back entrance of the office. The door was locked and all the windows had steel security bars over them. Just then a tapping noise drew her to the end window, and by the light of her torch, she saw Nancy's terrified face pressed against the pane. But Maggie could see that even if she managed to break the glass, there would be no way of getting the dratted woman out through the bars. She made a sign that she was going around to the front.

This was a wasted exercise. The front door was firmly shut, and the windows on either side barred like the back ones. By now the rain was running down her slicker and into her sodden shoes, and her feelings for Nat's ex-wife were making her even testier.

She returned to her car and took off around the block to look for a telephone booth. Quickly writing down the telephone number in large letters on her notepad, she zipped around to the back alley again and shone her flashlight onto the piece of paper so that Nancy could read it. She made a ten-minute sign and a dialing motion.

By the time she got back to the booth, the phone was ringing, but now there was a man inside the booth, sheltering from the rain, and he was about to reach for it. "That's for me," she yelled, wrenching the folding door open.

"Howdja know?" he answered, spewing alcohol fumes over her. "Could be for me," he slurred.

"Oh, for God's sake!" She pulled the man bodily from the booth, grabbed the phone out of his hand and kicked the door shut. "Nancy? What the hell are you doing in that place?"

"You've got to get me out before they come back."

"Can't you unlock the door from the inside?"

"I wouldn't bloody well be calling you if I could. The door's locked on the outside. Where the hell's Nat?"

"I haven't the faintest. Perhaps I should call the police."

"No! Get me out."

"Nancy, if I can't find a way in, I'll have to."

"I'll be charged with breaking and entering!"

"Okay! Sit tight." Maggie couldn't help grinning as she realized that Nancy had no other choice. Opening the booth's door, she pushed by the drunk, who had slid down to the ground and was fondly nursing from a brown paper bag.

Back in the parking lot, she sat in the car and surveyed the upper floor of the real estate office. There were no bars there, and although the two large windows were tightly shut, the small frosted one next to them that had to be in a bathroom was partly open. What she needed was a ladder. There were shed-like structures at the back of both the bookstore and the shoe repair shop, but there was also that glimmer of light coming from the bookstore itself, so she would have to try the shoe repair. Maggie pulled on a pair of gloves and climbed out into the rain again. However, the storage shed behind the shoe repair was tightly padlocked, its garbage cans in neat rows behind it and not a usable thing in sight. It had to be the bookstore's shed, light or no light.

Every step sounded like thunder as Maggie crunched her way across the gravel lot to peer into the shed—which thankfully was unlocked. Her flashlight revealed boxes, pails, jam jars and other accumulated junk, but high up on the wall, hanging on a couple of hooks, was a dilapidated wooden ladder. But just as she reached to unhook it, a dog began to bark.

"Shut up," a woman's voice yelled at the dog, and to Maggie's horror the back door of the bookstore was flung open and a strong beam of light suddenly focused on Maggie's car, then swept over the shed.

A woman stood in the doorway, clutching the collar of a huge black dog. "There's no one there, for God's sake. Just a car parked next door!" Minutes passed before the woman pulled the dog inside and closed the door.

Maggie waited a good five minutes before daring to briefly use her flashlight to locate the ladder again and then carefully lift it down. "Now the tricky part," she muttered. *Do I make a dash for it and hope I don't stumble or take it nice and easy?* The heavy ladder decided it for her, but her heart was in her mouth as she slowly crunched her way back to Nancy's prison.

She began to climb the wobbly ladder. The slightly ajar window hinged outward, but as the ladder only reached the bottom of the window, she would have to reach above her head to pull it fully open. Not daring to look down as she inched herself onto the top rung, she finally levered herself over the sill. Luckily, the toilet seat was down, because that's where she landed. The dull thud that followed was the ladder falling over, and the frantic barking was the dog next door. She quickly shut the window, felt her way to the door and headed downstairs.

It took a while to locate the room that Nancy was in, and unfortunately, there was no handy key in the lock. She tapped on the door.

"Is that you?" Nancy called.

*Who else would it be?* "I've got to find the key."

"For God's sake, make it quick." Nancy didn't know how near she was to being left where she was by a very wet, cold and bruised Maggie.

Eventually she found a board loaded with keys in what looked like a general office. They were probably keys to the businesses they had for sale as well as for the offices, but she gathered them all up and headed back.

"How on earth did you get locked in there?" Maggie asked as she began trying keys.

"There was no one at the reception desk when I came in, and I heard Mahaffy and Edgeworthy having a fight in his office. So I hid in here."

"Liam Mahaffy? How did you know it was him?"

"I met him at the Secret Valley lunch. How much longer are you going to be?"

"Cool it, Nancy. I'm going as fast as I can." As soon as she realized it wasn't a Yale lock, she was able to discard those keys before trying the others—one by one. "What were they fighting about?"

"That's what I was trying to hear, and then suddenly it went quiet, and that's when Edgeworthy locked all the doors."

Maggie was on the tenth or eleventh key when she hit the jackpot and Nancy stumbled out.

"Quick. Let's get out of here." Nancy, dressed in a bulky jacket and slacks, started for the front door.

"Not until I've replaced these keys," Maggie answered. "We don't want anyone to know we've been here."

"How would they know that?" Nancy answered.

"My car's parked out back and yours, I expect, is out front. Right?"

"So?"

"I've twice disturbed the dog next door, and they could quite easily have looked at my licence plates—or yours—while I've been rescuing you." She was about to close the filing room door when she had a sudden thought. "You haven't taken anything, have you?" she said, shining her flashlight on the bulging pockets of Nancy's jacket.

Nancy hesitated for a fraction of a minute before answering. "Why would I take anything? Come on! Put the damn keys back where you got them and let's get out of here!"

After relocking the file room door, Maggie replaced the keys on the numbered board. She would have loved to see the puzzled looks on the faces of the staff next day as they tried to sort them out. "Where do you live?" Maggie whispered before cracking the back entrance open and peeking out. No dog!

"Burnaby," Nancy whispered back. "Why?"

"Do you want me to follow you home?"

"What the hell for? Just give me a lift to where I've left my car."

"Where is it?" Maggie asked as she propelled Nancy to her Morris Minor.

"Outside that bookstore. There's no need to let Nat know about this."

"He has to know. You sure you didn't take anything?" she asked, unlocking the passenger door for her and noticing that both Nancy's hands were still jammed into the bulging pockets of her rain jacket.

"You calling me a thief? Just get me to my car."

They got to Nancy's car without mishap and Nat's ex-wife hopped out and made a beeline for it. Maggie, relieved to be rid of her, only waited a few seconds before pulling out into the road. Giving a last look back in her rear-view mirror, she saw Nancy waving at her to stop.

"Not on your life," she muttered. "I've had enough of you for one night."

"SHE DID WHAT?" NAT exploded the next morning. "You're telling me that my hare-brained ex-wife broke into someone's office?"

"Actually, it was Edgeworthy's Real Estate office." And Maggie gave him the details.

"You should've left her there," he said after she had finished. "Imagine what would've happened if you'd been caught climbing in that window? The police would've been all over us."

"That's another thing," Maggie said slowly. "You see, the damn ladder fell over when I was climbing in the window, and what with the rain and the dog next door barking—I just left it where it fell."

"Oh, that's great! Did the owner of the dog come out to see what was going on?"

"Only when I was getting the ladder down from the wall."

Nat groaned. "Hell, Maggie! Did he see your car?"

"It was a woman and she turned her flashlight onto it. But I was parked quite a distance away. I'm sure she wouldn't recognize it again."

"I hope so, for your sake. Are you sure you didn't disturb anything in the office?"

"Only the keys, though I probably put them back on the wrong hooks. And I was wearing gloves."

"Let's hope they weren't in any particular order." Nat sat back in his chair. "Well, we'll know soon enough if Edgeworthy realizes that someone broke in and the police start checking with the neighbours. Better get your notes, Maggie, and let's go over everything again."

"There is one other thing, Nat . . ."

He raised an inquiring eyebrow.

She pulled a small packet out of her pocket and slowly unwrapped it. "I found it on the passenger seat of my car," she added. "Nancy must have dropped it."

"Wow!" Nat exclaimed as he took the exquisite silver and turquoise bracelet out of Maggie's hand. "Where could she have got that?"

"It could be hers," Maggie said slowly.

"She could never afford anything like this."

"That's what I thought—and Nat, her pockets were bulging when she came out of that file room. I asked her if she had taken anything and she got all huffy."

"Oh damn," Nat said. "She's up to her old tricks."

This time it was Maggie who raised an inquiring eyebrow, but Nat didn't explain. Instead, he carefully rewrapped the bracelet and placed it in his desk drawer. "I think I'll get it appraised before I tackle her about it. But why would a piece of jewellery be in the file room of Edgeworthy's office?"

"Nat," Maggie said slowly, "I've been wondering—could that bracelet be Jacquelyn's? And if Nancy did find it in Edgeworthy's office, does that mean he's the one who burgled Jacquelyn's house?"

"Edgeworthy?" Nat said. They considered this idea in silence, then Nat said what they were both thinking. "Edgeworthy was Dubois's partner in the Secret Valley scheme, and it's possible he was the real estate agent who sold Maurice Dubois that house . . ."

There was a tap on Nat's door and Henny poked her head in the office. "Your old wife is here . . ." But Nancy pushed past her before she could say another word.

"Why didn't you stop last night?" she demanded of Maggie. "I dropped my bracelet in your car!"

"If you're talking about the bracelet I found on the passenger seat this morning, I've given it to Nat."

"Well, lover boy, you can hand it over. It's mine."

"Where did you get it?" Nat asked. "It looks very expensive."

"An admirer. He's not a cheapskate like you."

"If it's as expensive as it looks," Nat answered her, "you'd better take more care of it. Here." He pulled the desk drawer open and passed the bracelet to her. "And what exactly *were* you doing in that office?"

"You ratted on me," Nancy snarled at Maggie, and then turning to Nat, she added, "And it's none of your goddamned business."

"Yes it is when you involve this office."

"Well, I won't be needing your services again," Nancy said tartly.

Maggie waited until they heard the outer door slam before she said with a hint of laughter, "So much for getting the bracelet appraised."

"I've got a horrible feeling that our Nancy is up to no good," Nat said.

NAT WAS LATE ARRIVING at the office the following morning. After giving a quick rap on Maggie's door, he poked his head in.

"So where have you been while I've been slogging away?" Maggie asked, leaning back into her chair.

"I did tell you," he said as he settled into one of the visitors' chairs. "I said I would check on logging permits. Anyway," he continued, "after a lot of runaround, I got the clerk in the government office to look up the files, and he said that the only mention of logging on Hollyburn was for three ski runs. If any other logging has been done, they would have had to apply for a licence from the Ministry of Forests."

"And did they?" Maggie asked.

"He didn't have access to those records."

"That's convenient," she answered, ironically.

## CHAPTER SIX

The next morning, Jacquelyn Dubois visited the office again. "My lunch engagement is cancelled," were the first words Dubois's widow greeted them with, "so I have come to learn if you have found my Maurice's antiquities?"

It was on the tip of Maggie's tongue to ask her how well she knew Nat's ex-wife and whether she trusted the woman, but Nat was quicker.

"Hardly, Mrs. Dubois," he answered. "You know we questioned both your cleaning woman and the gardener, but we don't have the authority to search their homes. Only the police can do that."

"No, I tell you. No police. I want you to find the bad people who take my *objets* and, of course, my *pauvre* Maurice's life."

"We are trying, but there is very little to go on. Are you sure you want us to continue?"

"*Oui, oui,*" she answered, gathering up her fur coat and her clutch purse. "What about Annette and that son of hers?"

"You mean your husband's first wife?" Maggie asked.

"She is very jealous. Perhaps she take it."

"And his second wife?"

"That one has no . . . how you say . . . guts. Isabelle is just like her."

She was almost out the door when Nat asked, "Was Maurice stationed in Egypt during the war?"

"That was long before I married him. I do not know."

"You know," Maggie said after Jacquelyn left them, "she has a point. We've been focusing on the gang that was at that fishing lodge. Perhaps we need to take a closer look at wives one and two."

"But you think Nancy picked that bracelet up in Edgeworthy's office, don't you? So he's got to be mixed up in it."

Maggie nodded. "But what if I've got it wrong? What if Nancy already had that bracelet in her pocket when she went to Edgeworthy's office? Maybe he had nothing to do with it. Maybe it's all just a bunch of coincidences. After all, we don't even know if he sold Maurice that house . . ."

"And maybe the bracelet wasn't even one of the stolen pieces . . ." The thought that Nancy might have got the bracelet from some admirer just as she said she had was very appealing to Nat.

"EGYPTIAN ARTIFACTS?" ANNETTE DUBOIS seemed very puzzled.

It was Saturday morning, and Dubois's first wife had reluctantly agreed to see them in her small first-floor apartment on Fifteenth Street in North Vancouver.

"Maurice never had any art collections when I was married to him," Annette continued. "Anyway, what would I do with stuff like that? Apart from selling it." She gave a harsh laugh. "You can see that dear Maurice left me well provided for," she added sarcastically, gesturing to her surroundings.

The apartment, although fairly new, was cramped with its sagging sofa and two overstuffed armchairs, a dining table, four chairs and matching buffet that had definitely seen better days.

But surprisingly, on the floor was a brightly coloured Persian-style carpet in excellent condition. Maggie wondered what the rest of the place looked like.

"Does your son live with you?" she asked.

"René? He moved out once he got himself a job."

"He worked for his father for a while?" Nat asked.

"Six months. Then Maurice kicked him out. Now he works in a garment factory."

"Bakhash's Ready Made?" Maggie asked sharply.

"That's it. On Powell.'"

"What made him decide on that kind of employment?" Nat asked.

"Someone Maurice knew. Only good thing he ever did for his son."

"Do you know your ex-husband's second wife, Edith?" Maggie asked.

"Oh yes. She was his secretary, but it happened to her, too." She laughed again. "He got himself a younger and prettier one—that little tramp Jacquelyn."

"I heard that she was a model before she married Maurice."

"Ha! The only modelling that one did was to take her clothes off. She was some kind of exotic dancer, probably striptease." She stood up to indicate that the interview was over.

It was nearly noon when Maggie and Nat left Annette Dubois and headed for a nearby family restaurant for a quick lunch.

"Well," Maggie said, reaching for the breadbasket, "what do you think of her remarks about her son?"

"You mean about him working for Bakhash? What made you ask her about that?"

"I thought I recognized him the day I went to interview Bakhash. I'm sure I told you about the young guy arriving in an old army Jeep."

"And you think that was René?

"I thought at the time that he might be the 'and son' of Bakhash and Son, but I'm fairly certain now that it was René. You know, when you come to think about it, he and Jacquelyn must be very close in age."

Nat nodded. "That could make for an interesting situation."

After lunch they headed back to the city over the Second Narrows Bridge, as Edith Dubois and her daughter lived on Grant Street. Maggie was immediately struck by the contrast between the two residences—Annette's miserable little apartment and Edith Dubois's two-storied, well-kept home with its neat front yard, crisp white lace curtains and freshly painted green front door. Edith, too, was a complete contrast and welcomed them in with a smile.

"I saw you at Maurice's funeral," she said after seating them in the living room, "so I suppose you noticed that I wasn't very nice to Jacquelyn, but she's such a little upstart." She stopped abruptly. "I heard she'd hired some investigators."

"Yes, she's asked us to look into Maurice's death," Nat said. "Also the theft of some Egyptian antiquities that Maurice owned."

"Egyptian antiquities? First I've heard of Maurice owning any Egyptian antiquities."

"How long were you married to Mr. Dubois?" Maggie asked.

"Fourteen years too long. The only good thing that came out of that marriage was my daughter, Isabelle." She reached over and took a photograph off a side table and held it out to them. "Lovely, isn't she? I expect you saw her at the funeral, too."

"She's still in school?" Maggie asked, handing the photo back.

"She's training to be a beautician. I wanted her to go to secretarial school like I did. That's what saved me when that bastard dumped me for Jacquelyn—I got myself a job with an insurance company. It's been a struggle, but I'm okay."

"Have you ever been to Maurice and Jacquelyn's home?"

She shook her head. "Why would I go there?"

"What about Isabelle?"

"The odd time. The last occasion was Maurice's birthday bash last fall." She looked directly at Maggie. "And there's no way that my daughter would steal anything from that bitch, in case that's what you're thinking."

"YOU KNOW," MAGGIE SAID, "I'm beginning to wonder if those priceless antiquities ever really existed. After all, neither of the previous wives knows anything about them, and all we know about them is the pictures Jacquelyn showed us. What if this is just some kind of insurance scam that Jacquelyn is trying to pull off?"

"But she'd need the police to verify the theft if she was going to pull something like that off, and she's adamant that we not involve the police." He drove in silence for a few minutes and then added, "And besides, Nancy said she'd seen the stuff."

There was silence again as they both tried to decide whether Nancy's word was worth considering.

Suddenly Maggie glanced at her watch. "I'll need to do some shopping if we're going to eat in tonight."

She shivered as she got out of Nat's car at the Overwaitea store. Not one for grocery shopping, he opted to stay in the car while she battled the afternoon shoppers on her own. The sunny day had turned cold and blustery, and she couldn't wait to get inside the warm store and out of the cold. Valentine's Day was only a week away, and gaudy boxes of chocolates had now replaced the Christmas and New Year's promotions.

By the time they got to Maggie's house, it was quite dark. Nat, carrying the bags of groceries, followed Maggie up to her front door. There Maggie, balancing a bag of dog food on one hip, reached into her purse for her key, then froze in mid-motion. The door was ajar.

Pushing the door fully open, she rushed inside and then stopped. The place was a complete shambles. Chairs had been overturned and cushions ripped open, their contents spewed on the floor. The china cabinet had been emptied and the last of her precious ornaments lay broken. The kitchen was even worse. Canisters of rice, flour, tea, coffee and sugar had been emptied and tracked over the floor. And the intruders had left a message in red paint on the wall: 'Return the stuff. You won't be so lucky next time.'

Emily and Oscar were nowhere to be seen. Dropping the bag of dog food on the kitchen table, Maggie rushed up the stairs, calling their names. The drawers of her dressing table had been emptied and lay upside down; their contents were in heaps on the floor and mixed with all the bed linen that had been stripped from the bed. Hearing a faint meow, Maggie knelt and looked under the bed to see a crouched and miserable Emily. But there was no sign of the dog.

She walked slowly back down the stairs and into the kitchen, where Nat was on the phone to the police. "My bedroom! It's a mess! And I can't find Oscar."

"He'll be back," Nat said reassuringly as he replaced the receiver. He put his arms around her. "Poor little mutt. He must have been scared out of his wits."

"But why?" Maggie asked. "What do they mean—return the stuff? What stuff? Oh my God!" She suddenly remembered Nancy's bulging pockets.

That was the same question that Sergeant Hallscroft asked when he arrived. "Another one of your cases?" he added, setting a kitchen chair on its legs and sitting down. Maggie recalled that he had been the investigating officer on their last big case, when a young girl had been left for dead on her doorstep. "You two should choose better clients. Is anything missing?"

"Not as far as I can tell."

"What are you and Mrs. Spencer investigating?" Hallscroft asked, turning to Nat. "You've obviously touched someone's nerve."

"Several things. But the main one is looking into Maurice Dubois's death."

"Dubois? Where have I heard that name?"

"His body was found on Hollyburn," Nat answered.

"Ah, yes. I remember. But what has his death to do with," he looked up at the wall, "the stuff?"

"I don't know," Maggie answered miserably. "Perhaps they've got us mixed up with someone else?"

Hallscroft shrugged. "Could be mistaken identity, I suppose. I don't think there's any chance of us catching who broke in," he added, getting to his feet. "We'll ask around the neighbours, of course. You never know . . . one of them might have seen something suspicious."

"What about fingerprints?" Maggie asked.

"Not much point, really," he answered as he walked to the front door. "Probably used gloves. You did say there was nothing missing?"

"As I said, I don't think so, and my jewellery, such as it is, is still intact on my dresser upstairs."

"So we can clear up this mess?" Nat asked.

"Don't see why not. I think the thugs were giving you a warning, Mrs. Spencer. Perhaps you should heed it and choose another career," he said, walking to the door and opening it. "We'll keep an eye out for the dog," he added.

"If this really has something to do with that Egyptian

stuff . . ." Maggie began as she swept the last of the canister mixture off the floor. She stopped suddenly, dustpan in mid-air. "Nat, the bookstore."

"Bookstore?"

"Yes. When I rescued Nancy. I told you that I parked out the back and the woman from the bookstore came out to investigate. She could have told Edgeworthy about my car."

"But this mess would only make sense if Maurice's collection of Egyptian stuff really was stolen by Edgeworthy, and then Nancy came along and swiped the smaller stuff and put it in her pockets . . ."

"And if the woman from the bookstore told Edgeworthy about my car and he figured I'd stolen the stuff and he sent thugs to search my house."

"But we already decided that scenario was pretty far-fetched."

"Yes, but . . ."

It was at that moment that they heard a scratching at the back door. When Nat opened it, a bedraggled dog with a cowardly look on his face slunk in.

"A fine kind of watchdog you are," Maggie said, bending to pick him up and bury her face in Oscar's silky fur. "But I'm glad you're safe."

"Those thugs were definitely looking for something small," Nat said much later, as he sat on the side of the bed.

"What makes you say that?"

"The way your things were just dumped on the floor and the drawers turned upside down, and then both of your jewellery boxes emptied onto the dressing table and the contents spread out like that."

"And it's not all junk," Maggie said slowly. "There's my grandmother's two rings, this gold bracelet I've had for years and my gold watch . . ." She opened the clothes closet, picked up the pile of clothes from the floor and threw everything in. "I suppose Harry was right."

"Harry? What's he got to do with it?"

"He was dead set against me having the Morris Minor repainted red. Said it was too conspicuous."

## CHAPTER SEVEN

Thursday morning brought snow flurries to the Vancouver area, and Oscar loved it! Floppy ears and feathery tail flying in the icy wind, he bounded along happily with a huge grin on his face.

"It's okay for you," Maggie told him as she huddled into her fur-collared wool coat, "you're a typical Quebecois." But by the time the walk was over, even she was glowing and she actually found herself smiling at all the other dog-walkers. Reality set in again as soon as she removed her coat and surveyed the mess. Nat had done his best to clean up before leaving late the night before, but it was a bitter reminder of how dangerous her job could be.

*You've had worse things happen to you, Maggie old girl.*

With this thought in mind, she donned an apron and started on the kitchen floor. A couple of hours later, everything sparkled—she had even cleaned the inside of the kitchen window and refilled the canisters and put them back on their shelves—but try as she might, the words painted on the wall were still a faint reminder of the intruders from the night before.

"Paint or wallpaper?" she asked the two animals who were watching all the cleaning activity with trepidation. She would decide after she had tackled the bedroom.

"Perhaps I should take a day off more often," she said to Nat when he called her around noon to see how she was getting on. "And I have decided on wallpaper."

"Wallpaper? What the heck are you talking about?"

"To redo the kitchen walls. I'm going out to buy some this afternoon."

"Oh, Maggie," he groaned, "I'm not very good at wallpapering. All that sticky paste stuff. Let's just repaint."

"You've no need to worry. I've done it before."

"Somehow," he replied, "I have an awful feeling that I'm not going to escape that easily. You'll be in tomorrow?"

"Of course. Is everything okay?"

"Jacquelyn left a message that she would like to see us as soon as possible. I'll get Henny to set up a time."

After replacing the receiver, Maggie had a leisurely lunch and then went shopping for wallpaper. She chose white daisies on a yellow background.

THE NEXT MORNING, VANCOUVER awoke to a two-inch blanket of snow. When Maggie reached the office, Nat announced, "We'll take the Chevy to Jacquelyn Dubois's house. My tires are better than yours in this weather."

When they reached the house on Southwest Marine Drive, the flagstone path leading up to the ornate double front door had not been shovelled.

"Guess we're the first to visit her this morning," Maggie observed, looking down at the virgin snow. She stopped for a moment to look around the large garden. "Oh, Nat, just look how all the trees and bushes sparkle!"

He glanced at his watch. "It's twenty after eleven. You'd have thought someone, say the maid, would have left footprints." Then he laughed. "I bet there's a back entrance for the help."

"Are we considered *help?*" Maggie asked as she rang the front doorbell for the second time. "You did tell her eleven?"

"Perhaps we'd better try the back," Nat said after Maggie had rung once again. Stepping off the porch, he turned and stood looking at the house. On the left was the two-car garage and on the right the flagstone path led around the side of the house and up to a vine-covered latticed fence and latched gate. Nat led the way to the right. "Ugh!" he yelled suddenly. The path was close to the house, and a gob of the rapidly melting snow had plopped wetly from the eaves and down his neck.

There was no response to their repeated pressing of the back entrance bell either. "Where the hell is the woman?" Nat stormed. Then, in exasperation, he tried the door handle. It was open. "Mrs. Dubois," he yelled. "Mrs. Dubois, are you there?" He turned to Maggie. "That's it! I'm not wasting any more time. Come on." He closed the door and started back the way they had come.

"Perhaps something's wrong," Maggie answered. "I think we should have a look."

"She's probably gone out and forgotten we were coming."

"No, Nat. Ours are the only footprints."

"She could've gone out before the snow started."

"But it didn't start snowing until after midnight."

"Well then, maybe she's staying with a friend."

"And left the house unlocked? I don't think so." She turned the door handle and stepped into the immaculate kitchen. "Well, she had dinner here last night," she said, pointing to a couple of china plates, two empty wine glasses and some cutlery that had been left to dry on a rack. "But there are no breakfast dishes."

"We're trespassing, Maggie."

"Something doesn't feel right. I'm going to look through the rest of the house." Before Nat could stop her, she had opened the door into the large hallway and proceeded to the bottom of the winding stairs that led to the second floor. "Mrs. Dubois, are you all right?"

The only sound was the ticking of the huge walnut grandfather clock, which just then chose to play half of the Westminster chimes. It was now eleven thirty.

"I'll take a peek upstairs while you look over the ground floor."

"Maggie, I don't like this." He had just finished checking the living room when he heard her call his name. She was standing at the top of the stairs.

"Nat," she said quietly, "you'd better come up here."

Jacquelyn lay on her beautiful satin sheets in a pool of blood. The walls and even the ceiling were splattered with blood.

"She must've put up one hell of a fight," Nat said as he pulled a white-faced Maggie into his arms.

"How could there be so much blood in such a small human being?" Maggie asked, and her whole body shuddered.

"Let's go down and see if we can rustle up some brandy. Then I'll call the police."

"THEY MUST BE RECRUITING kids fresh out of school," Nat remarked fifteen minutes later, as he stood in the open front door watching two young officers park their vehicle in the driveway and walk toward him.

"You the one called in about a fatal accident?" The first one asked as he flipped his badge.

"It's no accident," Nat replied. "I'm afraid that Mrs. Dubois has been brutally murdered."

"And you are . . . ?"

"Nat Southby, and this is my associate, Mrs. Spencer. The body's upstairs. I'll show you."

"I can find my own way. You two stay here with my partner."

Nat shrugged. "Please yourself. But it's pretty messy." And he walked over to sit beside Maggie on the hall bench.

A few minutes passed before the ashen-faced cop appeared at the top of the stairs, his knuckles white as he held firmly to the rail. "Carter," he yelled, "call the station and get homicide here. And you two stay put. You've got some explaining to do." The wailing of an ambulance cut into his words, and as Carter opened the front door, they saw the vehicle pull into the driveway.

He turned to Nat. "Did you call them?"

Nat nodded. "Of course."

"You're too late, guys," Carter greeted the two attendants. "The lady's dead."

"We have to make sure. Where is she?"

"Follow me, but don't touch anything. We're waiting on homi . . ." He stopped in mid-sentence as a middle-aged woman pushed past the ambulance attendants.

"What's happened?" she cried.

"And you are?" Carter asked.

"I work for Mrs. Dubois. But my husband was ill and . . ."

"Mrs. Dubois is dead," he said brusquely.

"Dead?"

"Look," he answered her. "I've got enough to do. Go find somewhere to sit."

Maggie put an arm around the distraught woman and led her into the sitting room. "I'll explain things to her."

The quiet house that Nat and Maggie had entered that morning was now full of bustle, noise and cops. Two homicide detectives and the medical examiner arrived, followed quickly by a forensic team. As time went by, the ambulance and the two young patrol cops departed and the maid, having given a statement, was allowed to go home. Two hours later, Maggie and Nat were still waiting to be interviewed. And then suddenly there was a new arrival—George Sawasky.

"Am I glad to see you," Nat greeted him.

"What've you two been up to?" George said after shaking hands with Nat and giving Maggie a hug. "Can't keep out of things, can you? So what's happened here?"

"The dead woman happens to be a client," Nat explained. "Sit and I'll give you a brief rundown."

"And she called you yesterday?" George commented after Nat and Maggie had filled him in. "And you had no idea what she wanted?"

"We haven't made a lot of progress on either her husband's death or the break-in," Maggie explained. "I thought perhaps she wanted to call off the investigation."

"What break-in?"

"She told us she was robbed of some very valuable old jewellery and antiques."

"Did she go to the police?"

"No," Nat answered. "She absolutely refused. So you can imagine we've been a bit stymied on that front."

"Did you ever see any of this stuff?"

"It was stolen soon after she hired us to look into her husband's murder, but she did show us photographs of it."

"Where'd she keep the photos?"

"In the library," Nat said, getting to his feet. "On the other side of the hall."

"Lead the way," George replied. "There's not much I can do upstairs until the scene of crime officers are finished."

The album was still on the library table and it took them only seconds to find the photos of the Egyptian objects. "I'm not much on these kind of antiques," George said as he peered closely at each photo, "but these things look like the stuff you see in museums."

"Exactly," Maggie agreed. "Objects like this *are* only seen in museums, so if they *are* genuine, they would be priceless." She paused to gaze more closely at one of the pictures, a worried look on her face. Then, quickly turning to George, she said, "Jacquelyn told us that most of these things were displayed in Maurice's den." And she led the way down the hall. "She said most of them were on those shelves but some were kept in the safe over there. She figured that the thieves had got in through the French doors, but we couldn't find any sign of a break-in."

"I'd better get the special crime guys in here, too," George said before leading the way back to the living room.

"Is it okay for us to leave now?" Maggie asked, sliding up her coat zipper.

"Don't see why not. Of course, you'll have to come in and sign statements," he added. "And you'd better be prepared for Farthing to get into the case once he hears who found the body."

Nat groaned. Meetings with Farthing never did go well.

"I guess we're out of a job," Maggie said once they were outside.

"Guess so. But," he added, "now that we're out of the house, what was it you recognized in those photographs?"

"Didn't you see it, Nat? The bracelet. It's the one Nancy left in my car. I recognized the tiny beads threaded between the gems."

He sat thinking for a moment. "Perhaps Jacquelyn really did give it to her."

"Now you're dreaming," Maggie answered. "Nancy dropped that bracelet in my car after I rescued her from Edgeworthy's real estate office, and I'm absolutely sure now that she found it in that file room. And she had more of the stuff in her pockets, because she acted evasive when I asked if she had taken anything. She probably just took all the small pieces that would fit in her pockets."

After a moment of silence, Nat said slowly, "If you're right, Maggie, she could be in real danger."

"But Nat, it was my car that was seen outside the place, not Nancy's. And that's why it was my house that was trashed. Edgeworthy thinks I've got the stuff!"

Nat nodded. "Yes," he said, "you're right. But Nancy won't be able to resist flashing that bracelet around, and sooner or later the wrong person is going to spot it," Nat said vehemently. "We're going to find out exactly what she's up to."

But Nancy didn't answer her phone when he called her from the office, and when they drove to her house on Grasmere Avenue in Burnaby later that evening, they found it was shut up tight.

"I wonder where she is?" Nat muttered as he pulled away from the curb.

"DO YOU WANT ME to follow you home and stay the night?" Nat asked Maggie when they arrived back at their office. "I don't put much faith in Oscar protecting you."

Although Maggie was tempted, she knew they would keep rehashing everything over and over, and what she really wanted was to be on her own to think things out. "No, they won't come back, Nat. They know the stuff isn't at my house." Then, after promising to lock all her doors, she headed home to her own quiet dinner with Emily and Oscar.

EVEN THOUGH THE NEXT day was a Saturday, Nat received a call from Inspector Farthing's office demanding that he and Mrs. Spencer come in to see him right away. It had been over eight years since Nat left the force, but he still felt a slight twinge of nostalgia when they entered Farthing's office, because at one time it had been his own domain.

"So you two are still dabbling in police business," Farthing greeted them, indicating the two visitors' chairs. "And," he said, turning to Maggie, "you're back to your bad habit of finding dead bodies."

"Seems to go with the territory," she answered, smiling.

Farthing grunted.

"So what do you want to know?" Nat asked.

"For a start, how you two managed to be the first on another murder scene."

"I explained all that to Sergeant Sawasky."

"Well, you can just explain again," he said, reaching for his telephone. "Constable Goodwin," he barked, "I need you in here to take notes." And a few minutes later, to the surprise of both Maggie and Nat, a smartly dressed female police officer walked in, pen and pad in hand, and sat down beside Farthing. He turned back to Nat and said, "Okay, let's hear your story."

Nat began, "Jacquelyn Dubois engaged us to look into the death of her husband, Maurice . . ." And, being careful not to give too much of their investigation results away, he filled Farthing in.

"And what about this robbery?" Farthing asked when Nat had finished.

"We haven't been able to get too far on that either."

"Good thing, since you've lost your client." Farthing was smirking as he got to his feet. "We'll take it from here, so keep your noses out of it. And," he added, nodding toward the officer taking notes, "you can go after you've both signed the typed statement."

"Well that's one for the book," Nat said an hour later as they were leaving the station. "Farthing is actually allowing a police-woman to do his office work for him!" He gave a chuckle. "There's hope for him yet."

## CHAPTER EIGHT

When Monday morning rolled around, Maggie and Nat were both back in the office as usual.

"I guess we can put all the paperwork on Maurice Dubois's death away," Maggie told Henny as she gathered up the files.

"No client, no money," Nat commented. "But I'm still determined to have that talk with Nancy. I called her several times over the weekend without any luck. In fact," he said, as Maggie followed him into his office, "I didn't have much luck with you either. Where were you?"

"I told you I was going to visit Midge," she replied, closing the door so that Henny wouldn't hear. "I needed to get away for a bit."

"From me, you mean?"

"You know better than that, Nat. No. Jacquelyn's murder really got to me—that and the break-in at my house. Midge and I did girl things, like painting our toenails and shopping. Did me the world of good."

The Nancy problem was soon solved, too. It was getting toward noon when a very pale and frightened Nancy walked into the Southby and Spencer Agency.

"I can't believe Jacquelyn's dead," Nancy announced as she flopped into a chair in Nat's office. "Who would do such a thing? Oh, Nat, I'm so frightened."

"Surely there's no need for you to be frightened," Nat said as he signalled Henny to bring coffee.

"But who killed her? Do you think it was the same people who killed Maurice?" she asked, tears and mascara streaking down her face. "Perhaps I'm next."

"Why would you think that? You hardly knew the woman . . . unless there's something you haven't told me?"

"No, of course not."

When Henny entered and placed two cups of coffee in front of him, Nat pushed one of the cups toward Nancy and told Henny, "Ask Maggie to join us, will you?"

"Why do you need *her* in here?" Nancy was getting back into form.

"There are things *we* need to know," he answered, "such as where did you get that bracelet?"

"Why do you keep on about that? I told you it was a present."

"It's an exact replica of one that was stolen from Jacquelyn's home," Maggie said as she entered.

"Are you accusing me of stealing again?" Nancy demanded, jumping to her feet. "I come here for some comfort from my . . . my husband, and this so-called assistant of yours is accusing me of stealing."

"Where did you get it, Nancy?" Nat demanded.

"Jacquelyn gave it to me," Nancy blurted.

"Why would she give you something as valuable as that?" Maggie asked very calmly.

Nancy hesitated for a moment. "She said it was . . . it was just a fake. And . . . and it was too heavy for her to wear, anyhow."

"But," Maggie insisted, "you dropped it in my car after I rescued you from Edgeworthy's office. What was it doing in your pocket?"

"Oh, for God's sake," she exploded. "It was too heavy for me to wear, too." And flouncing out the door, she snarled, "A fat lot of help you are, Nat!" The door banged shut behind her.

After a few moments of looking at the closed door, Maggie sat in the chair Nancy had vacated. "Do you believe her?" she asked.

"Not in a million years," Nat answered with a snort. Reaching over his desk, he took one of Maggie's hands. "You're wondering why I married her, aren't you?"

"It did sort of cross my mind," she answered.

"I think I've told you that George Sawasky and I were rookies at the same station."

Maggie nodded. "You've been friends for a very long time."

"We were young, single and pretty impressed with ourselves in our uniforms. Nancy was a waitress at the greasy spoon where we used to have lunch. She was really quite pretty then—sort of cute, you know—and we both flirted with her, but for some reason she preferred me."

"Must've been your charming personality," Maggie said, smiling.

Nat shrugged. "Anyway, George wasn't really interested because he'd already met and fallen hard for Lucille. For a time we'd date as a foursome, but the two girls never really got on." He let go of Maggie's hand and leaned back into his chair. "Then George and Lucille got married. And you can guess the rest."

"Nancy wanted to get married, too."

"Yep! She wanted the whole works, big church, white gown, bridesmaids and of course, me in uniform. I realize, looking back, that she loved the uniform more than she did me. But she soon found out that being a cop's wife was no bed of roses—late nights, me being called out at all hours, poor pay. She was always on to me to quit the force and go into business like my brother. Things just went from bad to worse . . ." He paused to see if Henny would pick up the jangling telephone in the outer office. And a few moments later, there was a tap on his door.

"That nice boy René on telephone. He and his sister want to come in to see you tomorrow. I told him two o'clock. Okay?"

"WE WANT YOU TO continue investigating Dad's death," Isabelle said as soon as they arrived.

The last time Nat and Maggie had seen Isabelle Dubois, she had been hidden under a black veil at her father's funeral. It hadn't prepared them for the young woman they met now. Isabelle was tall and long limbed, her ash-blonde hair tied back in a ponytail, today dressed in a blue suede miniskirt and jacket. She was candy-box pretty but had the most startlingly beautiful blue eyes that Maggie had ever seen. Her stepbrother, René, was a complete opposite. His hair was chestnut brown, his skin darker, he was at least a couple of inches shorter than his sister—and he was definitely the young man she had seen getting out of the Jeep in Bakhash's parking lot.

"We know that he'd got himself mixed up in some logging scam," René began, "and maybe that could've been the reason he was killed." He turned toward his sister.

"Do you know what this scam was?" Nat asked interestedly. "Anything to do with Hollyburn Mountain?"

"You know about it, then?" Isabelle exclaimed.

"Not everything. Perhaps you should tell us."

René inched forward in his chair. "He got a legitimate licence to cut three ski runs on Hollyburn for this ski resort he was going to build, but he managed somehow to get somebody in the Forests Ministry to turn a blind eye while he logged half the mountain and a big chunk of Cyprus Mountain while he was at it. Made himself some big bucks."

"I take it this 'turning a blind eye' was the result of a bit of ready cash from your father," Nat said.

"Afraid so," René answered guiltily. "Actually," he added, "I helped him do some of the clear-cutting on Hollyburn—it didn't work out. I found it impossible trying to work for him. I'm not defending him; I just can't see why anyone would kill him for it?"

"Perhaps that wasn't the reason," Nat said, doing his usual doodling on the yellow scratch pad in front of him. "In any case, it wouldn't explain why your stepmother was killed a few days ago."

"Maybe that had something to do with Dad's collection of Egyptian stuff that was pinched," Isabelle said. "But who would want that old stuff anyway?"

"It's apparently extremely valuable," Maggie explained. "Museum quality pieces, from what we've seen of it . . ."

"So we've come to you," René butted in, "to find out who killed them. And Mr. Schaefer feels the same way."

"Mr. Schaefer?" Maggie asked, mystified.

"You know, Arnold Schaefer," Isabelle chimed in. "The man that Dad was in the lumber business with."

"Anyway," René continued, "he understands how we feel, because he offered to put up the money so that you can continue looking into Dad's murder . . . and I guess Jackie's, too."

"And find that Egyptian stuff," Isabelle added.

René put his hand into his coat pocket. "He gave us this cheque to give you as a retainer. Will it be enough?"

Nat was stunned. He was looking at a cheque for five hundred dollars. "More than enough! All right, we'll continue working on it. Mrs. Spencer will take you into her office and get you to sign the necessary contract." He reached over his desk and shook their hands. "We'll do the best we can."

Maggie escorted them to her office, and while she filled out the contract form, she remarked, "I'm really surprised that

Mr. Schaefer is helping with the finances. He didn't seem to care about your dad's murder when we saw him just before the funeral."

"That's just his way," Isabelle answered. "He's a real softy inside."

Maggie nodded. "I see. Now I just need you two to sign here . . . and here." As she watched them sign, she found herself making a mental bet that it was Isabelle with her beautiful blue eyes who had persuaded Schaefer to hand over the money. Then she asked, "You work for Jerrel Bakhash, don't you, René?"

"How do you know that?"

"I saw you driving into his parking lot the day I went to interview him."

"Yeah! I was at a loose end last fall and Dad got the job for me. But I'm thinking of quitting."

"You're not happy there?" Maggie asked.

"It's okay. But I don't see myself cutting out shirts forever and . . ." He hesitated, looked toward Isabelle and then continued, "There's something odd about the place."

"What kind of odd?" Maggie encouraged.

"Well, I started working in the packing room . . . you know, opening crates of cotton and stuff, but every time these two guys showed up with their truck, Bakhash always wanted me to run an errand or do something upstairs for him."

"What kind of guys?"

"Well, I think they're brothers, and they have funny accents. And sometimes a big guy who looks like their father comes with them."

"What kind of funny accents?" Maggie persisted.

René thought for a moment. "They're English accents, I guess. Not the la-di-da kind, but you know . . . And then suddenly Bakhash transferred me upstairs to the cutting room."

"Maybe Mr. Bakhash realized you had more potential," Maggie said.

"René shook his head. "No, I think I got too curious."

"Perhaps they're just retailers picking up their orders."

"I suppose. But why so secretive?"

Maggie walked them to the door. "Would you give me a call if you see or hear anything else you think is odd? But," she added as she handed over her card, "do be careful."

"You mean you want René to spy on them?" Isabelle asked excitedly.

"No. I just want him to be alert to what's going on there."

"Oh, and about Mr. Bakhash," René said as he was halfway out the door. "I'm supposed to be at the dentist this afternoon. I'd rather he didn't know I was here."

"Fine with me," Maggie answered, shaking his hand. "Keep in touch." When she shook hands with Isabelle, she couldn't help but notice that the girl had a ring on nearly every finger. *Well, she may not have cared for her stepmother, but she certainly shared her love of jewellery.*

"SO," MAGGIE SAID AFTER telling Nat of her conversation with the brother and sister, "I'd say that the guys with the funny accents sound very much like Henry Smith and his two charming sons. What do you think?"

"I think you're right, and they're up to some kind of monkey business with Bakhash. And what about Schaefer paying for our services?"

"He's the last person I'd expect to cough up the money for us to continue." Maggie shook her head in wonderment. "He certainly wasn't what I'd call welcoming when we went to see him. Perhaps he is, as the Dubois kids say, all bark and quite a softy inside."

"Well, it's back to interviewing and shaking a few people

up—especially Bakhash. And," he said, waving Schaefer's cheque, "the Southby and Spencer Agency is going to treat its two top investigators to dinner at Monty's tonight."

"And they deserve it," Maggie replied.

NANCY EMPTIED THE CONTENTS of the paper bag onto her dressing table, then reached for the ornate gold earrings and put them on. A turquoise and gold necklace and a heavy matching bracelet were next, and she preened first one way and then the other while she surveyed her reflection in the triple mirrors. If she squinted a little, she looked exactly like the pictures of that statue they found before the war of that Egyptian queen, Nefer-something-or-other . . . although the statue had been a little skinnier.

Then, one by one, she picked up each of the other bracelets, rings and necklaces, trying them on and studying the effect in the mirror. "They're a trifle on the heavy side for my taste," she told her reflection. "But if the gold and silver are real, they're worth a mint." Nancy didn't have a clue what some of the other objects were—they looked like carved lumps of stone—but she picked up one and then another and looked at them closely. One was a heart-shaped, speckled green stone with a beetle deeply carved on top; another was made of glazed pottery with symbols of some kind carved on the underside. Placing them back on the dressing table, she reached for the last piece of jewellery, an armlet made out of wood with ivory inlays. She pushed it as far as it would go on her right arm, stepped back from the mirror and preened once again.

Taking a cigarette out of a crumpled pack, Nancy slowly lit it and took a deep drag. It was obvious to her now that these were some of the Egyptian artifacts that had been stolen from Jacquelyn. There had been lots more sitting right there in boxes in Edgeworthy's file room, but most of it had been too big to go into her pockets. But what the hell had it been doing in there in the first place? And was that why Jacquelyn had been murdered? It was a frightening thought. But she soon brightened up. "They have no way of knowing I was there. And," she laughed, "if anyone can be tied to the break-in, it'll be that conniving bitch in Nat's office." Still wearing the jewellery, she walked into her kitchen, took the telephone book out of a bottom drawer and thumbed her way through the yellow pages. "Ah, here we are—antique dealers."

# CHAPTER NINE

Valentine's Day brought two surprises for Maggie. The first was a heart-shaped box of her favourite chocolates, which Nat had placed on her desk, and the second was the delivery of a dozen red roses. "My goodness, Nat has really gone overboard," she said as she took in their heavenly scent. "Especially," she added, "as I only gave him a card."

"Here," Henny said from the doorway, "I haf brought vase."

Maggie placed the small gift envelope that had fallen out of the bouquet onto her desk blotter before carefully placing each bud into the vase.

"I hope that's the right kind of chocolates," Nat said from the doorway. "And thanks for the card." He stopped suddenly when he saw the roses. "You've got another admirer?"

"You mean you didn't . . ." Maggie quickly opened the envelope and then sat down abruptly. *Your wedding bouquet was roses*, she read, *so I know how much you love them. Harry.* "Oh, dear," she said.

Puzzled, Nat walked over to the desk and picked up the card. "He never gives up, does he?" He turned and walked out of the room.

"Oh, Harry," Maggie said quietly, glancing at the calendar. They would have celebrated their twenty-ninth anniversary last Saturday.

FRIDAY WAS GREY AND very windy. Maggie, driving along Hastings Street, had to grip the steering wheel firmly as the strong gusts slammed against the side of her small car. She was thankful when she eventually turned into Bakhash's parking lot.

"As I told you on the telephone," he said, escorting her into his office, "I can only spare you a few minutes."

"I appreciate you giving me the time," she answered, settling into the comfortable seat and taking out her notepad. "You know about Jacquelyn Dubois's murder?"

"So sad. A waste of a beautiful woman."

"You knew her well?"

"No. I have already told you that I met Maurice at the fishing lodge. He was trying to sell property there."

"But," Maggie answered as she turned the pages back on her steno pad, "you employed Dubois's son."

"And what business is that of yours?" he asked tightly.

"You told me that you met Dubois for the first time at the fishing lodge. And then I find out that you employed his son last fall."

"And may I ask how you know that?"

"I saw him entering the building on my last visit, and his mother told me he was working here."

"I was doing the boy's father a favour."

"But you only met his father at New Year's."

Jerrell Bakhash glared at Maggie through his horn-rimmed glasses. Bending towards her over his huge desk, he growled, "I do not want to be mixed up in a bloody murder. So I lie! I met that man at a dinner last fall, and he did nothing but carry on about his son. I offered to help by giving the boy a job."

"And the ad in the paper for investing in St. Clare Cove?"

"That is true, but I knew about it beforehand. Now, you excuse me?" He walked around his desk. "Tell me, madam," he added as he ushered her through the door. "I can't see you detective people doing this for free—so now that the widow's dead, who is paying you?"

Maggie was saved from answering, because Bakhash's secretary was frantically waving the telephone toward him. "It's your call to Cairo."

Bakhash grabbed the phone and began an animated conversation in Arabic. As she walked out into the corridor to descend the stairs, Maggie leaned over the rail to see the rows of women she'd seen on her last visit, heads bent over their sewing machines.

WHEN NAT ARRIVED BACK from lunch, he found his friend George Sawasky chatting to a delighted Henny while he sipped a mug of tea and munched on one of her monster cookies. She had been making these cookies for Nat from the first week of her employment with the agency. They were always burnt or overdone and as hard as nails. Nat hated them, but George actually seemed to be enjoying the things.

"Thought I'd drop by and see how you're all doing," he said, tossing the last of the cookie into his mouth.

"I've kept one for you, Mr. Nat. I'll bring it with your tea."

"I had a late lunch, Henny. Wrap it up for George to take home with him." Quickly escaping into his office, he indicated for his friend to follow. "Any news on Jacquelyn's murder?" Nat asked.

"Not much. We know that she died as the result of multiple stab wounds to the throat and upper body. The pathologist's report states that the fatal blow was to the heart."

"She put up a fight?"

George nodded. "There was bruising to the neck and arms and both her hands were deeply cut."

Nat thought for a moment. "I guess the killer could have tried to restrain her by holding her by the neck," he said slowly, "and the cuts to her hands point to her trying to ward off the knife. Do you think there was more than one attacker?"

"I suppose there could have been. Hey!" George said suddenly, "Why the interest? Your client's dead."

"We've been hired back again," Nat replied, laughing. "But don't worry, you haven't given too much away." Both men turned to the door as Maggie entered.

"What hasn't he given away?" she asked, giving George a hug before sinking into the other chair. "What great secrets have you been letting slip?"

He repeated what he had told Nat. "So who's rehired the pair of you?"

"Actually it's the son, René, and his stepsister, Isabelle," Maggie told him.

Then Nat asked, "Do you think you could keep this fact from our friend Farthing?"

"I won't volunteer the information, but he's bound to find out," George said, getting to his feet. "And," he added, "a little bit of exchange of information wouldn't go amiss. I'll be in touch." He walked into the outer office. "Bye, Henny," they heard him say. "Nat's so lucky that you make him such good cookies."

"That rat!" Nat muttered. "Now she'll make masses more."

"Anyway," Maggie said suddenly, "we know that Jacquelyn knew at least one of her callers that night. Remember the dinner dishes on the drain board?"

"I wonder if they found any fingerprints on them," Nat said, drawing his yellow pad toward him. "How did the interview with Bakhash go?"

"I've got the feeling he's one very dangerous individual," Maggie said, looking down at her notes and filling him in on what she had learned.

"So he lied about knowing Maurice Dubois," Nat commented.

"Have you got the original list of people who were at that resort?"

Maggie flipped back the pages of her notepad and passed it over to him.

"So," Nat said, drawing his yellow pad toward him, "Bakhash now admits to knowing Maurice before the New Year's get-together. Schaefer was his partner in the lumberyard. Robert Edgeworthy was his partner in the Secret Valley ski resort deal. The Smiths say they didn't know him, but Jacquelyn said that Dubois had called at their emporium a few times." He paused, pen in air. "The last on the list is Liam Mahaffy, and he was in the army with Schaefer but says he only met Dubois in Pender Harbour."

"And into the midst of this motley crew," Maggie said, grinning, "comes your ex-wife, Nancy, and the bracelet and whatever else she stole that night from Edgeworthy's office. What we don't know is why all that stolen stuff was in Edgeworthy's office in the first place."

"You're absolutely sure she came out of there with more than the bracelet?" Nat asked.

"Her pockets were bulging when she ran for my car and she kept her hands jammed into them as if she didn't want the stuff to bounce out. You don't suppose she would try to unload the stuff at a pawnshop or an antiques dealer?"

ROSIE SMITH HELD THE bracelet in her hands. "Where did yer get this?"

"A gift from a dear friend," Nancy answered. "She told me it was genuine Egyptian."

"Don't know about that," Rosie answered, taking it over to the light. "Good replica. Give you seventy-five bucks for it."

"It's worth at least a hundred and fifty."

Rosie drew in a deep breath and let it out slowly. "Not much call for this type of thing. But out of the goodness of my heart, I'll give yer a hundred—my last offer." She opened the till and drew out five twenties.

"Okay," Nancy said reluctantly. This was the third place she had tried that afternoon and it was her best offer yet.

"Any more where that come from?" Rosie asked casually as she handed over the money.

Nancy looked straight into the other woman's eyes. "No," she answered and turned and walked towards the door. But what she didn't see was the nod that Rosie gave to one of her sons, who was polishing a table nearby. And unknown to Nancy, she had acquired a shadow as she sauntered down the street to where she had parked her car.

## CHAPTER TEN

Oscar was one happy dog. Saturday dawned clear and spring-like, so that afternoon Maggie and Nat took him for a long walk in Stanley Park. He got to chase his favourite Frisbee on the grass and sticks on the beach, but he absolutely refused to go into the cold sea for them—he wasn't that stupid! After sharing a hot dog from a vendor in the park, he graciously allowed his favourite people to take him home, where, after giving Emily the cat a wet slurp, he crawled into his basket and fell asleep.

"There are some good movies on this weekend," Nat said, reading from the newspaper. "There's one of those funny English movies—*Carry On Regardless*, a horror movie with Audrey Hepburn called *The Children's Hour* and a western, *Gunfight In Black Horse Canyon*. Take your pick."

"Not the western," she replied with a shudder. "That name . makes me think of Black Adder Ravine, where that woman took a potshot at me."

"And I wasn't there to save you. Anyway, to get back to the movies, I'm not too keen on the Audrey Hepburn one, so let's have an early supper and go and see Sid James. We both could do with a good laugh."

The movie was great fun and they were still laughing about

it on their way home. "There's nothing like a good British comedy," Nat commented as he parked the Chevy in front of Maggie's house.

"But you know, with all those British accents, right in the middle of the movie I suddenly found myself thinking about Henry and Rosie Smith."

"And you asked yourself what Bakhashes' ready-made clothes have got to do with the Smiths' fake antiques, right?"

Maggie took off her coat and went into her small kitchen to put the kettle on. "That's the problem. I can't make a reasonable connection, except that they were together last New Year's at the fishing lodge."

"Perhaps it's time that I went for a browse in the Smiths' emporium," Nat said as he took two cups and saucers out of the cupboard.

MAGGIE LOVED TO WAKE up on Sunday mornings to the smell of coffee wafting up the stairs. Nat's brew always tasted better than anything she made, and then there was the added smell of bacon. She made it downstairs just as he placed the two plates laden with eggs, bacon and toast on the kitchen table. "I think I'll keep you, Mr. Southby," she said, giving him a kiss.

"You'd have a helluva job getting rid of me now," he answered, handing her a mug of the coffee and watching her take an appreciative sip. "And I'm ready to make it permanent whenever you give the word."

"I know," she answered. "I know." But Maggie also knew in her heart that she wasn't ready to make that commitment. "I'm going to Barbara's this afternoon," she said, changing the subject.

"Yes, you told me," he answered. "It's your grandson's fourth birthday." He always felt left out of Maggie's other life with her family. "I suppose Harry, the giver of roses, will be there," he added grudgingly. He knew that Harry would do anything to get Maggie to go back to him.

"He *is* Oliver's grandfather."

"I know." He rose from the table and came to put his arms around her. "I'm sorry for sounding so jealous."

THE BIRTHDAY PARTY WAS in full swing when Maggie arrived at the door with an armful of presents for her only grandchild. When she followed Barbara into the living room, a beautiful family scene was laid out before her. Her son-in-law Charles sat on the floor, holding little Oliver on his lap as they watched a Hornby 00 gauge train whiz around an oval track. Equally entranced and kneeling on the opposite side of the track was Jason, Midge's old boyfriend, and sitting in a cretonne-covered armchair with a self-satisfied look on his face was Harry, who was obviously the giver of the train. Maggie realized that her presents of a Pooh Bear, books and puzzles were superfluous. There was no way she could compete with a train.

"Hello, Margaret." Harry pulled himself out of his chair and came to greet her with a peck on the cheek. "Glad you could make it. Thought you would be too busy detecting."

"Wouldn't miss my grandson's party for the world." Maggie was determined to keep things light. Nothing was going to spoil Oliver's day.

Hearing her mother's voice, Midge, who had been helping Barbara in the kitchen, ran into the room and gave her mother a big hug. "Here, let me help you with your things. Look, Oliver, come see what your grandma has brought you."

"There's plenty of time," Maggie said, sinking down into the other armchair. "Let him enjoy his train."

Later, after an over-excited Oliver had been put to bed, the adults chatted over their coffee.

"Lovely party," Jason said, snuggling up to Midge on the sofa. "But I suppose you're surprised to see me, Mrs. Spencer?"

"I was too polite to ask," she answered with a laugh.

"He persuaded me that I couldn't live without him," Midge said. Maggie had always liked Jason and had been very sorry when the two had split a year earlier.

"And what about the other good news?" Harry chimed in.

"What other good news?" Maggie asked, looking around at everybody.

"Oh, Father, I haven't . . ."

But before Barbara could finish, Harry cut in, "Hasn't Barbara told you? She's making me a grandfather again," he said smugly.

Maggie felt a cold shiver run down her back. "No. I guess she hasn't," she replied. She looked at her elder daughter. "I'm so pleased for you and Charles."

"Mother, I *was* going to tell you. But I was so busy with Oliver's party and I didn't want to break the news over the phone and you're always so busy . . ." Her voice trailed off.

"So when is the baby due?"

"Late September."

Maggie's feelings were hurt, but she knew her daughter's actions weren't without some warrant. Barbara was very close to her father and Maggie *was* always busy, and that fact couldn't help but make the rift between them worse.

# CHAPTER ELEVEN

Nat drove past the Exotic Eastern Emporium on Pender, looking for a convenient parking spot. As he started to walk back to the store, he took a deep, appreciative breath. It was a beautiful Monday morning, and spring couldn't be far off, as there was a definite lift to the air. Unfortunately, it was fast intermingling with exhaust fumes, but that was the price one paid for being in this part of the city.

Pushing open the door of the emporium, he was immediately faced with a smell of a different kind—a mix of mouldering bric-a-brac, furniture polish, dusty carpets and incense. Looking around, he had to agree with Maggie that although he didn't know too much about antiques, most of the merchandise seemed to be a load of junk.

"See anything you like, dearie?" Nat realized that this overly made-up, peroxide blonde must be Rosie.

"These are not genuine?" he said, pointing to two tall vases masquerading as cloisonné.

Rosie seemed to size him up before answering. "I can see a gent like you knows a real genuine article when he sees one."

Nat nodded wisely while he studied a small lacquered inlaid table. "But this piece is," he said, keeping his fingers mentally crossed.

"Original from India."

"What I'm really looking for," Nat said, wending his way past several delicate-looking tables laden with bowls and vases, "is something Egyptian. But it has to be authentic, as it's for my wife's birthday, and she's been reading that new book about King Tut's tomb."

She studied Nat for a moment. "Hard to find and very costly." She paused before she asked, "Is it jewellery you're after?"

"Jewellery or a small object. And don't worry about the cost."

"Give me your name and phone number. I'll see what I can come up with."

"It would be better if I called you," Nat explained. "I want it to be a surprise."

"I'll need a few days," she said, leading him to the counter at the back of the store. "What did you say your name was, ducky?" she asked, her pen poised over a huge order book.

*Oh, hell!* His gaze settled on a Chinese screen. "Harvey Peacock," he improvised. The "Harvey" was legit, as it was his hated middle name.

"Lovely name," Rosie said, handing him a business card. "Here's our phone number. Give me a call later in the week."

IT WAS ALMOST ELEVEN by the time he reached the office and poked his head around Maggie's door.

"How did the party go?"

"Okay, I guess," she answered. "Harry bought Oliver a train set."

"The little guy must have loved that," he said, coming all the way into the room. "But what gives me the feeling you're not too happy about it?"

"Oh, Nat, it's not the train set. It's just that I got the awful feeling that I didn't belong." She couldn't stop the unbidden tears that sprang up.

"What did that man say to upset you like this?" He pulled Maggie to her feet and wrapped his arms around her. "Was he his usual pompous self?"

"Barbara's having another baby, and Harry knew and everyone else knew but no one had told me," she said, her voice ending on a sob. She tried to pull herself away from his arms. "I'm being silly and I need a hankie."

"Use mine. And you aren't silly. I'd like to give that family of yours a good talking to. Now," he said gently, leading her back to her chair, "you sit tight and I'll fetch you a cup of coffee, and if you like," he added, his eyes twinkling, "I'll even persuade Henny to give you one of my cookies." But when he did return, he had fresh coffee for the two of them and the bag of doughnuts that he'd bought on his way back from the Smiths' emporium. He soon had her laughing as he related his visit to the store and especially his choice of *nom de plume*.

"I'M OFF TO VISIT the alluring Rosie," Nat called out to Maggie the following Wednesday morning.

"Don't mortgage your flat buying exotic jewellery," Maggie answered with a laugh. She was trying hard to push away the blues that had clung to her since Oliver's birthday party.

"I'm only going to look at it." Nat had called Rosie Smith and been told that she had managed to put her hands on a lovely piece, and could he come in around eleven? "What are your plans for the day?" he asked Maggie, who had emerged from her office to collect her coat from the rack in the reception area.

"I'm going to do some very necessary shopping, but I'm meeting with Donald Black at Smedley and Smedley at two o'clock for instructions on the new case they want us to investigate."

"Did he say what it's about?"

"Something to do with an adoption agency. But I'm not sure if we have the time to take on anything else at the moment."

"Get the facts and we'll discuss it later. Okay?" Shrugging into his overcoat, he opened the outer door for her. "The place is all yours, Henny."

ROSIE SMITH SEEMED DELIGHTED to see him. "I see you're a gent that keeps his word," she said, leading him to the back of the store. "You'd be surprised how many people make arrangements and then don't bother to turn up." She reached behind the high counter and brought up a small object wrapped in tissue paper. "Now this is one of a kind," she said as she unwrapped it.

Nat believed her. The last time he had seen that bracelet was when Nancy snatched it from his hands. He picked it up and pretended to look at it closely. "How much?"

"Twenty-five hundred. A bargain for a gent like you." She took it from his hands. "The faience tells you it's genuine, see?"

"Faience?"

"They're these little blue-green beads that are threaded between the turquoise. The old Egyptians always stuck them in between semi-precious stones."

"How old is the bracelet?" Nat asked reverently, taking it back into his hands.

"Could be around 2000 BC."

"Wow," he said, genuinely impressed. "How did you come across it?"

"You'd be surprised what comes across this counter," she answered evasively. "But like I said, it's a genuine Egyptian queen's bracelet."

"And you want $2,500 for it?"

"I could come down a bit . . . say, $2,250."

He hesitated for a fraction of a minute. "And you're sure it's genuine?"

"I'll stack my life on it, Mr. Peacock. I know my antiques."

Nat was sure she did. "Make it $2,000," he said rashly, "and it's a deal."

Rosie pondered for a few moments before holding out her hand. "Cash only. We don't take no cheques."

"I don't keep that kind of money on me," he said. *In fact, I don't even have that much in my bank account!* He opened his wallet and took out the two fifties he had withdrawn the day before. "Will this hold the bracelet?"

Rosie took a deep breath and let it out slowly. "Well . . . it's not much. But seeing how you're wanting it for your wife, I'm willing to hold it for a couple of days."

"She'll love it." And he managed to exit the Exotic Eastern Emporium without actually running.

WHEN MAGGIE FINALLY RETURNED from her afternoon appointment, Nat recounted his adventure with Rosie Smith.

"And you're sure it's the same bracelet?"

"Absolutely. She went into a long spiel explaining what the little blue-green beads are—Egyptian faience—it's some kind of ceramic."

"I wonder how long it's going to be before they realize that you used a fake name and that Nancy is your ex-wife?"

"Might be a while, as she usually goes by her maiden name— Gladstone." Nat was quiet for a moment. "But of course, if the Smiths are working closely with Robert Edgeworthy, they know perfectly well where she found that bracelet."

"I'm sure they're in it together," Maggie answered. "And with Nancy busy selling off the loot she stole, they'll soon be after her to find out where she's stashed the rest of the stuff."

Nat reached for the phone. "I've got to warn her, Maggie." He let the phone ring for at least two minutes before replacing the receiver. Then, glancing at the wall clock, he said, "We have to get over there."

"PERHAPS SHE'S GONE SHOPPING." They had rung the bell several times, walked around to the back of Nancy's house and banged on the rear door. Still there was no answer. "What about the neighbours?"

"Fat chance that anyone could see what's going on here," Nat answered, indicating the tall cedar hedges growing on either side of the house. "Nancy always liked her privacy. But it's worth a try."

The neighbour on the right was a woman with a very young family. "We're on our way to the park," she explained to Maggie as she strapped the youngest of her three children into a stroller.

"We wondered if you'd seen your neighbour, Mrs. Gladstone, around?"

The woman shook her head. "I only know her just to say hello." She gave a tight smile. "Don't think she's into kids."

As Nat approached Nancy's other neighbour's house, the lace curtains in the front window twitched. Lifting up the horse's head door knocker, he gave a sharp rat-a-tat and waited. Eventually, a grey-haired woman cracked open the door and looked out enquiringly. "Yes?"

"Just wondered if you've seen your neighbour, Mrs. Gladstone, around lately?"

"You mean that woman next door?" She nodded toward Nancy's house.

"I've tried several times and there's no answer. Did you happen to see her go out?"

"She's always going out."

"I mean, today?"

"No. You the cops?"

"No. A friend." Nat tried not to show his irritation as he turned to go back down the steps.

"There were two men parked outside in a big grey car early this morning."

Nat swivelled around to face the woman. "How early?"

"It was still dark. Maybe around five o'clock."

"Did they go into the house?"

"Yeah!"

"How do you know the car was grey?"

She looked witheringly at him. "It was parked under the street light. Then I saw one of the men get back into the car and drive off." She lowered her voice and whispered, "Don't know what happened to the other man, but that woman's no better than she ought to be ... if you know what I mean. Comings and goings all night."

"But you didn't see Nancy, Miss ... ?"

"Mrs. Mable Maggs. My Albert crossed to the other side fifteen years ago. And I'm not a busybody like some people." She shut the door, but as Nat started down the front path, he saw that she had taken up her vigil behind the curtains once again.

"We have to get into Nancy's house," Nat said when he rejoined Maggie and told her about the grey car. "Suppose she's in there hurt or something?"

"Or it could be as the old girl said and the visitors are legit." Then, seeing the look on Nat's face, she continued hurriedly, "How do you propose we get into the house?" Secretly, she thought that Nancy didn't deserve rescuing again.

"We'll try the back again. Maybe there's a window open."

There was no open window. But while they were debating their next step, Maggie had a thought. "Nat, what about her car?"

"Right! Her car." And not waiting for Maggie, he strode down the path to the wooden garage. The doors were firmly shut and locked, but by standing on tiptoe he managed to peer through a small dust-covered window to see that the car was still safely inside. "Yeah, it's there," he called back to Maggie, "so something's happened to her—she wouldn't go anywhere without her car. We've got to get into the house."

Maggie began expertly wrapping a large stone in her scarf. "I think we're going to have to break in." But there was no need to break in, as the back door had been left unlocked. "This doesn't look good, Nat. You'd better go in first."

The kitchen was a shambles of emptied canisters, cupboards and drawers. Apart from the torn sofa cushions, the living room had hardly been touched, but the upstairs was another matter—clothes in piles, drawers gaping open, closets emptied, the mattress tipped up on its side and the bedclothes in a heap. The bathroom had suffered a similar fate, as there were cosmetics strewn over the floor amid pills and lotions from the medicine cabinet. It was obviously the work of the same *artistes* who had worked over Maggie's house.

"I wonder if they found what they were looking for," she said.

"They've got Nancy, by the look of it," Nat answered gloomily, walking through the chaos. "I could wring her bloody neck for being so stupid. The old biddy next door said she only saw one man in the car when it was driven away," he said thoughtfully. "My guess is that he drove around the back and they smuggled her out that way."

"Let's go and have another look at the backyard." Maggie moved toward the door. "And it wouldn't hurt to talk to a few more neighbours. And what about the police?"

"They'll only ask awkward questions." And he followed Maggie out the back door.

It was obvious that Nancy was not a gardener. Trampled weeds surrounded an old birdbath and the sagging remains of a tool shed, and overgrown shrubs lined the cracked cement path that led to the garage and back alley. Freshly broken twigs on the bushes lining the path suggested her unwilling passage through them.

Later the two of them sat in Nat's Chevy, deciding what they should do next. "I think we should call George," Maggie said at last. "There'll be hell to pay if we don't report her apparent kidnapping."

"It's Nancy landing in jail for pinching that Egyptian stuff that I'm worried about."

"Then," Maggie answered slowly, "let's keep that to ourselves for a while. Tell George that Nancy asked you to call on her, and when there was no answer you got worried and we broke in."

"George is not going to buy that," Nat answered with a snort.

"He can suspect all he wants," Maggie answered, "but we've got to really delve into this business between Smith and Edgeworthy, and we don't need the police getting in the way." When Nat finally agreed with her strategy, they returned to Nancy's house to use the telephone.

Of course, George didn't buy their story. But when Nat insisted that whatever Nancy wanted to see him about was strictly private, he had to accept their version of events.

"But who would want to kidnap her?" George asked after the forensic team had arrived to thoroughly search the house. "Has she been getting herself into something nasty or illegal? You must have some idea."

"The only thing she came to me about was to get me to help Jacquelyn Dubois find out who killed her husband."

"It all seems very fishy," George commented. "This doesn't have something to do with your house getting tossed, too, does it, Maggie?"

Before Maggie could answer, Nat cut in quickly with, "We don't know, George. We just don't know."

"Okay," George said. "You two can go now, but I'll be around to see you in the morning. And Nat," he added, "I hope Nancy is not mixed up in something illegal and you're shielding her because she's your ex-wife."

IT WAS VERY LATE in the afternoon when they returned to the agency. Henny had already left for the day, leaving a scrawled message on Maggie's desk. *That boy with funny French name called, said he needed to speak to you urgent. Henny.*

"If it's urgent," Maggie said, "I'd better call him right away." She pulled René's file to look up his telephone number, but although she tried several times before they left the office, there was no answer. "Well, he'll call again if it's really urgent."

THE TWO OF THEM were sitting over a take-out chicken dinner in Maggie's kitchen.

"The problem is that we don't know which one of them took her," Nat said.

Maggie could tell that, even though Nat was thoroughly exasperated with his ex-wife, he was still worried about her. "It has to be the Smiths," she replied. "Nancy went to them with the bracelet, so they must realize she has the rest of the missing stuff. But we can't just go to the emporium and ask if they have her."

"No." He fidgeted with his fork. "Same thing goes for Edgeworthy. Where does he live, anyway?"

"Twin Oaks Drive, Gleneagles. I remember the address because it sounded so expensive," she explained as she reached for the phone book to check the house number.

"You're right! It's where the money is," he answered wryly. "It's in West Vancouver near that yacht club," he said with a glance at the kitchen clock. "But it's after seven and it's already dark."

"It's the dark we need," Maggie replied, gathering up the plates. "Let's at least go and see if Edgeworthy owns a grey car."

## CHAPTER TWELVE

Nat drove cautiously along Marine Drive in West Vancouver as it twisted and turned in ever-tightening s-bends. Twice he pulled over close to the rock face to let another vehicle pass them, and it was with a sigh of relief that they eventually emerged at the turnoff to Gleneagles.

"Now to find Twin Oaks Drive," he said as he pulled over and directed a flashlight onto the map that Maggie held.

"We're very close. Let's leave the car and walk the rest of the way."

The house was situated halfway down a short, secluded and twisty road. It stood at least a hundred feet back from tall wrought iron palings and gates.

"Wow," Maggie said quietly. "This is some place. It must have a fantastic view of the ocean."

"It overlooks Batchelor Cove. I visited a client up this way a couple of years back," he explained. He gave one of the double gates a trial push and it swung inward with a rusty squeak. Grabbing Maggie by the hand, he pulled her through, swung the gate shut and followed her into the shadow of the trees lining the wide drive.

Light from the uncurtained downstairs rooms lay across the driveway, where it made a wide sweep past the front of the house before ending at a double garage. A flagged stone path separated the house from the garage. To get there, they would have to cross the lighted area.

"Ready?" Nat whispered. But just as he was about to take the first step, he felt Maggie tug him back into the shadows. "What?" Then he, too, heard the car stopping and the creak of the gates. "Phew! That was close," he breathed as they watched a black Buick purr past them, down the driveway and into the now open garage. The driver seemed to take forever to re-emerge, briefcase in hand.

"It's Edgeworthy." The two of them watched him walk to the front door, which was immediately opened by a small girl with a large German shepherd by her side.

Edgeworthy stooped and picked the child up in his arms, but the dog shot out into the night, barking and snarling.

"Come on in, Prince," the man called sternly. "He's after the damned squirrels again," he said exasperatedly. He put the child down inside the door. "I've told your mother repeatedly that animal needs obedience school. She never listens."

But the dog had caught the scent of humans, not squirrels, and to Nat and Maggie's dismay was making straight for them as they retreated backward into the densely wooded area.

"Prince!" Edgeworthy snarled as he followed the dog down the drive. "Get in here!"

The dog, hearing his master's voice, was in a dilemma— chase the engaging scent or obey. A further enraged yell from Edgeworthy and, to Maggie and Nat's relief, the dog turned and reluctantly went back to the house.

They didn't move a muscle until they saw Edgeworthy grab the animal by the neck and drag it inside. But even after the door was shut, they could still hear it barking.

"I'm glad it hasn't gone to school," Maggie whispered after a few minutes. "It might have been trained as an attack dog." A few minutes later, and breathing easier, they were on the other side of the garage. "At least we know he drives a black Buick."

"Perhaps she drives a grey one. Let's take a look." But unlike the gates, the garage doors front and back were firmly locked. It took Nat quite a few minutes to use his picklocks to get inside.

"You're a man of hidden talents," Maggie whispered. There was only room for two cars and the other one, which they surmised was Stella's, was an ordinary green Ford. "Well, we could've been lucky. But somehow I didn't think Nancy would have been stashed here, not with a small child in the house. Come on, let's go!"

They were almost back at the gate when the dog burst out the front door of the house again, barking wildly. "Christ! He's let that monster out again," Nat yelled. They made it through the gates moments before the enraged animal threw itself frenziedly against the wrought iron, and despite his size, Nat was not far behind Maggie as they sprinted for the safety of the Chevy.

Their next stop was the Smiths' Exotic Eastern Emporium, but there were no lights showing either downstairs in the shop or upstairs in the Smiths' apartment. And there wasn't a sound except for the passing traffic.

"There's nothing more we can do tonight, Nat," Maggie said. "Let's go home and get some rest. We'll think better in the morning."

THE NEXT DAY STARTED with a meeting of minds in Maggie's office.

"So how do we find your old wife, Mr. Nat?" Henny demanded, settling into one of the visitors' chairs. They had already brought her up to date on Nancy's kidnapping. "I can go to that junk shop and see if she is there."

"Good grief, no!" Nat exclaimed in horror. "We have to approach this very carefully."

"I am very good at detecting, Mr. Nat."

"You know, Nat, Henny could be right," Maggie said thoughtfully. "There was nothing to see there last night, but we've still got to nose around the Smiths' place in the daylight to see if they own a grey car, and neither of us can do it, because the Smiths know us."

"No," Nat said emphatically. "If they're as dangerous as we think they are, Henny's not going anywhere near them. Besides, she's needed in the office today. I have to be in Victoria by two thirty this afternoon for that meeting with Forestry."

"Oh," Maggie said, "I'd completely forgotten. What ferry are you catching?"

"I have to be in Tsawwassen in time for the *Sidney's* eleven thirty sailing. What are you doing today?"

"I'm going to call on Arnold Schaefer's wife."

"Schaefer's wife? What would she have to do with Nancy's disappearance?"

"Maybe nothing. But I still think all the answers lie in Maurice Dubois's previous life."

"Do you mean when he lived in Montreal?"

"No. It's just that Jacquelyn told us that Maurice was in the army and so were Mahaffy and Schaefer. Perhaps that's where they met up."

"I see." Henny nodded wisely. "Mrs. Schaefer could let the cats out of the sack."

"Something like that, Henny," Maggie said, smiling.

"Well, it's worth a try, I guess," Nat said at last. "But we've got to find Nancy before any harm comes to her."

"We'll find her, Nat," Maggie said.

Sergeant George Sawasky's entrance brought their meeting to an end, and Henny immediately left to get him a cup of coffee and find him one of her specials.

"I need information fast," he said, plonking himself in the chair that Henny had just vacated. "No more stalling. Why was Nancy snatched? And don't give me any more BS that you two have no idea."

Maggie and Nat looked at each other and then Nat gave a sigh. "George, it's a bit embarrassing, considering she's my ex-wife. You remember the photos I showed you of the stolen Egyptian collection? Well, somehow Nancy's got her hands on one of the bracelets from that collection—and the long and the short of it is that the thieves want it back."

"Where did she get it?"

"We're not sure, but she showed it to us and insisted that Jacquelyn Dubois had given it to her." Then Nat went on to describe the bracelet turning up at the Smiths' Exotic Eastern Emporium, although he left out the fact that they were pretty sure that Nancy had stolen the bracelet from Edgeworthy's Real Estate office.

"So why tumble her house? What were they looking for?"

"I suspect the thieves think she has the rest of the stuff."

"There's got to be more to this," George frowned as he looked from Nat to Maggie. "How did this bracelet turn up at that junk shop?"

"Either Nancy sold it to them ... or they took it from her. And thereby hangs another sad tale," he said ruefully. "Rosie Smith is trying to sell it to me for two thousand bucks."

"Serves you right," George commented unsympathetically after he heard that his friend was out one hundred dollars. "I told you to keep me in the picture. And," he continued, "you two are still holding something back. Thanks, Henny," he said, taking the coffee and cookie from her, "you'll have to give my wife the recipe." Henny beamed with pleasure as she refilled their cups.

The look that Nat shot at George should have ended their friendship right then and there.

As soon as George had gone and Nat left to catch the ferry, Maggie told Henny, "I'm going to call Thelma Schaefer. Maybe she'll see me this morning."

MAGGIE TOOK THE SECOND Narrows Bridge to North Vancouver. Driving over the huge structure, she thought about the terrible tragedy only three years earlier when a large section of the bridge span had collapsed into the inlet, sending eighteen workers to their deaths. The new bridge had only been completed the previous year. Maggie still felt insecure each time she used it.

The Schaefers' door was opened by a comfortable-looking, middle-aged woman in a grey uniform, who showed Maggie into the perfectly appointed living room where Thelma Schaefer waited for her. Trim-figured, every hair in place and beautifully dressed—in fact, the perfect colonel's wife—she sat in her wheel-chair beside a tea trolley.

"So you're Mrs. Spencer," she said, smiling graciously and holding out her hand to Maggie. As Maggie's hand closed over it, she was aware how small and fragile the woman was, and she wondered what had put her into a wheelchair. An accident? Disease, perhaps?

"Maisie has already brought in the coffee." She indicated the trolley laden with a Royal Albert service and a tiered cake stand with small cookies and petites fours. "Now what can I do to help with your enquiries?" And she began pouring coffee.

"You're English, too," Maggie said, settling into a cretonne-covered chair on the other side of the trolley.

The woman nodded. "I guess you could call me one of the early war brides," she said, smiling as she handed Maggie a cup of coffee. "I met Arnold about ten years before the war. He was in London on some kind of hush-hush military thing. He never told me what."

"But he was in the tank corps during the war."

"Yes," she said sounding surprised. "The Middle East. How did you know that?"

"Liam Mahaffy. He seemed very proud to be part of your husband's outfit."

"Oh, dear Liam." She smiled. "Such a *nice* young officer."

"You met him during the war, then?" Maggie asked, taking a bite out of a cookie.

Thelma nodded. "Arnold and I had a lovely little cottage in Ashford. Sometimes he would bring one or more of his men home for a weekend. They appreciated that, as most of them were so far from home."

"Your husband obviously kept in touch with Liam. What about Maurice Dubois?"

"Maurice Dubois?" She looked puzzled. "Oh, Maurice wasn't in Arnold's unit. As far as I know, he was in a French Canadian regiment . . . the Van Doos." She reached over to the trolley to offer Maggie a petit four. "No, Arnold's men were all British . . . although he did bring a couple of Canadian offi-cers home once . . . they were on temporary duty with the 8th, although for the life of me I couldn't tell you their names any-more."

"Was one of them Robert Edgeworthy?"

Thelma Schaefer paused in the middle of refilling Maggie's cup. "Of course, you're quite right. Robert was seconded to Arnold's company when they were in North Africa," she said, passing Maggie the cup. "Do you know him?"

"We've met. He told me that he was at the lodge with your husband over New Year's."

"Was he? My goodness, I didn't know that."

"Was there a Henry Smith in your husband's company?"

"I don't know, dear. If he wasn't an officer, there was no way

I would have met him." Then she asked, "Was he a big man? A cockney, perhaps? Because now that I think about it, there could have been a Henry Smith in stores or something like that. Of course, it's such a common name." She reached for the little bell on the tea trolley and rang it. When the housekeeper arrived a moment later, she asked, "Maisie, could you bring me the photo on the Colonel's desk in his den?" While they waited for it, she continued, "So many of them were either killed or missing in action." She paused. "War is a terrible thing."

The photo turned out to be the same one that Liam Mahaffy had shown them. "So did you get to meet any of these others?" Maggie asked, taking it into her hands.

"Some. That's Liam, the one laughing in the back row. Such a clown," she added fondly. "And next to him is, of course, Robert. He was transferred shortly after that picture was taken. But we're so pleased that Liam came to BC to live," she continued. "He tried his hand at farming on Lulu Island, but his real love was always horses."

"He runs a stable in Delta now, doesn't he?"

"That's right. Arnold tells me that he boards and trains race horses there."

Thelma leaned across the trolley and took the photo from Maggie's hands. "More than half of them didn't make it back."

"I lost two of my cousins in the Battle of Britain," Maggie said. "I've never stopped thinking of them." They drank their coffee in silence for a few moments, then Maggie asked, "Was your husband in the lumber business before the war?"

"No. The lumberyard was Arnold's father's business. Arnold only went in with him after the war, and then his father died just a year later."

"Is that when your husband took Maurice Dubois on as a partner?"

"Maurice? Well, he wasn't really a partner, you know, and the only reason he was involved with my husband at all was because he persuaded him to expand into logging. Worst mistake Arnold ever made." She stopped abruptly, as if she had said too much.

"Then it was very thoughtful of him to finance René and Isabelle so that we can continue investigating the two murders."

"I didn't know he had." For a moment she looked almost shocked at this revelation, and then her usual mask of politeness returned and she added, "I'm a little surprised, as he wasn't exactly enamoured of Jacquelyn, but I guess he has a soft spot for René and Isabelle. Their father's many marriages have been difficult for them."

"You knew both his previous wives?"

"Not Annette. She and Maurice had divorced and he was already married to Edith by the time I came here after the war. But I must say this of him, he was very fond of both of his children and took a great interest in their growing up."

"I appreciate you seeing me," Maggie said, folding her small linen napkin, "especially on such short notice."

"I'm sorry I haven't been more helpful."

Outside, Maggie sat in her car for a few minutes before reaching for the ignition. "Oh, but you have, Mrs. Schaefer," she said quietly as she pulled away from the curb.

NANCY WAS TERRIFIED. SHE had been tied up and her mouth duct taped before she was dragged through her backyard in her nightgown and then thrown into the trunk of a car. At the end of the journey, she had been blindfolded, hauled out of the car, dragged up a long flight of stairs and interrogated again by the two thugs. She told them in vain that Jacquelyn had given her the bracelet and she had no idea where the rest of the stuff was, but that had only led to them slapping her around some more.

At last she had debated telling them that she had buried it in the back garden, but figuring they would kill her off once they had it in their possession, she had kept her mouth shut.

Now she was still tied up, but at least they had taken the blindfold off and left her alone in this small bedroom for a while. Tears coursed down her face at the indignity of still being in her torn nightgown with cold, bare feet and, worst of all, no makeup. She looked up fearfully as the door crashed open once again and a pile of clothes was thrown at her.

"One peep out of you and you get this," one of the men said, pointing a gun at her. Then he walked over to her and untied her arms. "Get dressed."

"Please let me go home," she whimpered as she pulled the grey sweatsuit on over the nightgown. "I won't tell anyone!" She reached for the knitted wool socks. At least her feet would be warm. "Please."

"Shut up," he said as retied her hands behind her back and reached for the roll of duct tape.

"Not the tape, please. I promise I won't say a word." But relentlessly he taped her mouth shut.

## CHAPTER THIRTEEN

"It's all very embarrassing, Mr. Southby." It was three fifteen on Thursday afternoon, and Nat was sitting opposite Jake Houston, a grey-haired, lean man in his mid-fifties. "It was your enquiries into that logging scam on Hollyburn that brought the subject to our attention . . . so we started to investigate ourselves." The Forestry official looked acutely uncomfortable.

"And you found that there was definitely something fishy going on?"

The man nodded, steepled his fingers and continued ponderously, "Yes, that clear-cut on Hollyburn was definitely illegal. And . . . it seems there are more large tracts of land—mostly in our wilderness parks on Vancouver Island and probably in the northern part of British Columbia—that may have been logged without our knowledge."

"How is that possible?"

"Because of the remoteness of the areas in question. There are rangers, of course, but these are vast areas we're talking about, and I'm afraid we have a few dishonest people in the business. That's where you can help us."

"Me?"

"We want you to make enquiries."

"Thanks for your consideration, Mr. Houston, but I haven't

the time to tramp all over BC looking at logging sites. And I certainly don't have the expertise to know whether they've been logged over their allotted boundaries or . . ."

"No, no. That's not what we're asking you to do. Your agency has already uncovered this Dubois character, but he's dead. What we need to know is who his contacts were in order to see if they lead into other nefarious goings-on in the . . . uh . . . ministry."

"What about the RCMP?"

"We must keep a low profile with this. We're approaching you because you are already on the ground floor of this case, so to speak. Besides, you are a former police officer and it's obvious you know your way around."

Nat sat quietly thinking about the money, the prestige and the possibility of future jobs with the government before he answered. "You understand that I have to consult my partner before I could agree, and that we would require the names and addresses of all your staff who could possibly be involved."

Houston nodded. "Then you will consider taking this on for us?"

IT WAS A LITTLE after five, and Maggie was preparing supper for herself. She hadn't heard from Nat so supposed he wasn't back from his meeting in Victoria. After popping one of her made-ahead pot pies into the oven, she was sipping a glass of red wine while waiting for her dinner to warm up when the telephone gave its annoying jangle. She debated letting the thing ring, but then it could be Nat or even one of her daughters. Placing her glass of wine on the counter, she reached for the instrument.

"It's René, Mrs. Spencer. I've been trying to get hold of you since yesterday afternoon."

"What's wrong?"

"You told me to call you if I heard anything unusual," he answered in an accusing voice. "Well, I did. I heard Bakhash and some guy yelling at each other."

"In the office?"

"No. The stockroom in the basement. I had to go down there to get a bolt of seersucker."

"Did they see you?"

"No, no. Anyway, Bakhash was yelling at this guy about him grabbing some woman and that there were better ways to get the stuff back."

"Did you recognize the man?"

"No, I couldn't see him, but the important thing is, Mrs. Spencer, Bakhash told him that another consignment would be coming in, and that they would be unpacking it Friday evening when there was no one around."

"You mean tonight?" Maggie asked.

"Yes, and this other guy said that at least my dad was no longer a threat, and if that fool Edgeworthy had followed instructions, the other stuff would have been safe, too."

"Good work, René! This is important information."

"Anyway, I could smuggle you into the building, and we could see what they're up to."

"Heavens no, René. That would be foolhardy to say the least. Remember, both your father and stepmother have been murdered . . . and probably by these same people."

"But I want to find out why," he answered vehemently.

"Mr. Southby would be dead against us doing any snooping." She paused for a moment while possibilities ran through her mind. "And I can't ask him, as he's not back from Victoria."

"You want to know what's in those crates, don't you?"

"Certainly, but this would be far too risky."

"Then I'll have to go by myself."

"You can't possibly go in there alone," she said. "What if you're caught?" Then she added reluctantly, "Oh, all right. But I'll need a safe parking spot for my car."

"There's a restaurant called the Daily Bread quite near the factory and it has a large parking lot."

"Okay. I'll meet you there." She replaced the receiver, grabbed her coat and turned the oven off. "I guess supper's going to be a mite late."

Maggie was still feeling very unhappy about the venture as she parked her car. Nat would be furious when he found out. She got out and was locking the door when René suddenly appeared at her side.

"I still don't think this is a very good idea, René," she said when she climbed into his old Jeep.

"Hold tight, Mrs. Spencer," he said as he swerved around the corner and both their seats shot forward. "Sorry," he said. "The seats have come loose on their runners."

"I see what you mean," she yelled at him over the noisy engine. "Why don't you get it fixed? That's really dangerous!"

"I keep forgetting," he said as he pulled the Jeep over to the curb just around the corner from the factory.

"Look, René," Maggie said as she clambered out of the vehicle, "if I feel that it is too dangerous for us to be here, we're leaving. Understood?"

"Okay. I understand."

The evening had turned cold and the harsh wind made Maggie pull up the fur collar of her wool coat. She buried her hands deep into her pockets, and her right hand closed around her trusty flashlight. "How do you propose we get into the building?"

"Don't worry. I've got this," and he brandished a large key. "My supervisor keeps it in his desk, so I borrowed it."

The grim, totally dark building did nothing to lift Maggie's spirits. She watched in trepidation as René fitted the key into the scarred wooden door. With the banks of sewing machines silenced for the night, it was eerily quiet inside. "Which way?" she whispered.

A beam from René's flashlight lit up the square reception area, and taking Maggie by the elbow, he led her to a door she hadn't noticed on her previous visits. It revealed wooden stairs leading down into inky blackness. "Be careful. These stairs are steep and they curve." Maggie brought out her own flashlight and followed him down, but she was relieved when she felt the solid floor beneath her. René played his flashlight over four rows of tall racks, their shelves piled high with bolts of fabric and enormous cartons of Bakhash and Son's shirts.

"What if they come back early?" Maggie whispered as she followed him between the racks.

"Oh, there are lots of places to hide," René reassured her.

About twenty feet from the freight doors, the racks ended, and much of the remaining space was filled with enormous empty cartons and wooden crates stacked in higgledy-piggledy fashion against the walls and the ends of the racks.

"See," René said, "there are the crates I was talking about." He played his light over three huge wooden boxes standing close to the freight entrance.

Maggie walked over to inspect them in the beam from her own flashlight. She could see right away that the wooden lids had been firmly hammered shut and that each crate had been tightly bound with thin metal strips. There was no easy way to open them. "What we need is a crowbar," she said.

"You're not going to open them yourself?" René asked in horror.

"How else can we see what's inside?"

"I thought we'd hide out until they came and opened them."

"I plan to be long gone before they get here, René."

"But if you open them, they'll know someone's been here."

"So what?" She swept the beam of her flashlight over the cartons, brought it to a halt on a workbench that stood against the far wall, then walked purposefully toward it. "This will do it," she announced and, picking up a box hatchet, headed back to the crates, jammed the blade under the metal strapping of the nearest crate and heaved. It gave a satisfying snap and fell to the floor. "This shouldn't take long," she said, as she got ready to break the next one.

"Oh, merdé!" René hissed. "Someone's coming."

"What?" Then Maggie heard the sound, too—cars arriving outside. "René!"

Taking Maggie by the hand, he pulled her toward the huge pile of carelessly stacked crates and cardboard boxes.

"I thought you said there were plenty of hiding places," Maggie hissed, tightening her grip on the box hatchet.

"There are," he whispered back, "but we don't have time to get there."

She put a hand up to steady the cartons before they toppled down on them. *One puff of wind and this whole lot will go,* she thought.

They extinguished their flashlights moments before the door rolled up. Peering between the boxes, they could see three men silhouetted in the entranceway. Maggie stifled a gasp when the sudden draft caught one of the boxes that had been balanced on the top of the pile and sent it skittering across the concrete floor. A moment later, the whole area was flooded in harsh light.

"Shut the bloody door," one of the men yelled. "It's freezing."

Maggie silently agreed. She could see her breath as she hunkered down on the floor next to René.

Just then the door rattled down again.

"Let's get this done," one of the men snapped. "Hey," called another voice, "what's this?"

There was silence for a moment and then Maggie recognized Henry Smith's voice "Must have been one your lads done it, Bakky," Smith said calmly.

"I gave strict instructions that no one was to touch these crates."

"Calm down, Bakky. You know people don't listen. Let's get 'em open."

"My name is Bakhash, Mr. Smith—Bakhash!" he snapped. A few minutes later, they heard a volley of Arabic and the sound of tools being flung onto the floor. "Where is that bloody hatchet?" he yelled in English.

"Oh, damn!" Maggie mouthed silently as she hugged the box hatchet to her chest.

"For God's sake, Bakky, get a grip!" Smith's voice seemed very close to their hiding place. "You must have more than one. Here, this'll do it . . ."

Maggie realized that she had been holding her breath. She only let it out when she heard the snapping of the metal strips breaking and then the screeching of nails as the wooden tops were wrenched off.

"Now, slow, slow . . . be careful with the fabric," Bakhash ordered. "I can't make shirts with torn and dirty cotton." Then a while later, "Okay, stop . . . stop there. Gently, gently . . . Put it over there."

Maggie signalled to René that she was going to take a peek and slowly got to her knees so that she could see between the boxes. René, struggling to rise beside her, accidentally kicked the metal flashlight that he had left lying on the floor.

"What was that?"

"Rats," Bakhash answered.

"It came from over there," Smith said.

"Come on, come on! Let's get on with it!"

Shaking with fear and the cold, the two in hiding could see Smith and another man dressed in a hooded jacket. They watched as the men withdrew long rolls of cotton from one of the crates, then held each roll vertically while Bakhash pushed cotton-wrapped packets—some of them only inches long, others much, much larger—from their cardboard cores. They repeated the same long process with the other crates before they slowly unwrapped each packet and laid the objects within them reverently on an overturned crate.

"We've hit the jackpot this time," the man in the jacket breathed, picking up what looked like a small ebony cat, from the way its jewelled eyes glinted under the light.

Maggie and René watched spellbound as the men picked up piece after piece and examined them before rewrapping them.

"Whew!" Smith said. "This lot's worth millions. And this time I'm taking charge of it," he continued. "We can't risk another blunder."

"It wasn't my fault that Gladstone bitch got into my place!"

*Edgeworthy!* Maggie thought. *I'm certain that's Edgeworthy.*

"She must have had help," Bakhash said, as he began reverently rolling each piece in cotton fabric. "Your neighbour saw that Spencer woman's car in the alley."

"What *looked* like her car," he corrected testily. "Anyway, your boys went through her place, didn't they? And they didn't find . . ." He held up his hand. "Sounds like someone's outside."

"Probably the boss. He said he would come and make sure everything was okay." Smith walked over to the freight door and scraped it open. "It's a good haul," he greeted the new arrival.

The gust of wind that accompanied the boss's entrance sent

more of the empty boxes flying. Maggie was thankful that she and her partner-in-crime had taken advantage of the interruption and carefully eased themselves inside two of the empty crates.

One of the men must have made a move to pick up the scattered boxes, because Bakhash shouted, "Leave them. I'll get them later."

Maggie would have given anything to have seen who this boss man was, but there was no way she was going to risk another peek.

"Everything intact, then?" From their hiding place inside the crate, the newcomer's voice was muffled.

"Smith's got buyers lined up," Edgeworthy answered.

"What about the woman?" the newcomer asked.

*I know that voice*, Maggie thought.

"Still says she only had the bracelet," Smith said, "and I'm beginning to think she's telling the truth."

The boss's response was too low for Maggie to hear, but Smith came back with, "Well, she only tried to hock the bracelet." Then he added, "Anyway, you gotta get her outta my emporium. I got a business to run."

There was a muttered response, probably from the boss, and then Smith said, "Okay, we'll take her to the farm tonight."

"Come on, let's get on with it," Edgeworthy snarled, "so we can get out of this freezing hole."

"Give me one of them little boxes to pack this stuff in," Smith said.

Maggie, holding her breath as she huddled inside her crate, listened as someone picked up one box after the other, discarding the rejects back onto the pile.

Finally Smith called out, "That'll do."

IT SEEMED AN ETERNITY before Maggie heard the freight door rattle up again, the overhead lights went out and the door rattled down. She felt René relax beside her, but they waited without speaking a word until they heard the cars depart before they struggled out of their cramped quarters. Their bodies were stiff from nearly an hour of tension and crouching, and their teeth were chattering with the cold in the unheated storeroom. They stumbled back to the stairs and out into the dark night—René carefully locking the door behind him.

"They're smuggling stuff into the country from Egypt, aren't they?" he asked as they piled into the Jeep. "And my father was somehow mixed up in it, too."

Maggie didn't answer until they were back in the parking lot and she was safely behind the wheel of her Morris. She rolled the window down to speak to René.

"He was either involved in the smuggling or he somehow managed to get his hands on some of the pieces."

"And after he was killed, those bastards took them back. What do we do now? Go to the cops?"

"We've no proof, René. Anyway, let me discuss this with Mr. Southby before we take any action. And keep this to yourself. Go back to work tomorrow as if nothing has happened."

"All right," he answered dubiously.

Still shivering from the cold, Maggie drove home and quickly turned on the oven again to reheat her pot pie before reaching for the telephone. *I've got to tell Nat about Nancy. He must be home by now.* But the phone rang before she could lift the receiver.

"Where the hell have you been, Maggie? I've been calling and calling."

"Nat! Thank God you called. They're holding Nancy at the Smiths' emporium, but they're going to move her out of there tonight, so we'll have to get there fast."

"How do you know?"

"I'll meet you there."

"But . . ."

"I'll explain when I see you."

When she'd hung up the phone, she turned off the oven again and rushed out to her car.

She was surprised how much traffic there was for nine o'clock on a Thursday evening, and it took a while to find a vacant parking spot a block from the Smiths' store. The rain that had begun as she was leaving home turned into a torrent as soon as she started to jog from her car toward the Exotic Eastern Emporium. Nat had managed to park his inconspicuous old Chevy across the street and a couple of stores down, and she could see him, oblivious to the rain, nervously pacing to and fro beside it.

"How do you know she's here?" he demanded when she ran up to him.

"I'll tell you later. We haven't much time. Come on!"

Not waiting to see if he was following, she took off for the intersection of Pender and Seymour and ran down the alleyway that would lead her to the back of the emporium. A truck had been parked a couple of stores short of the Smiths' shop. There was very little room between it and the back wall of the building, but by holding her breath, Maggie managed to squeeze into the gap between them and take a cautious look. The emporium's back door was wide open and the whole area was flooded with light. She could see Rosie and Henry Smith talking to two men beside a dirty brown van, which was pointing away from Maggie toward Richards Street. The engine was running and it looked ready to go.

Maggie backed out as quickly as she could, only to bump into Nat, who had been unable to push his bulk into the narrow space to be with her.

"What's happening?"

"Shh! There's a van and it's about to leave."

"Is Nancy in it?"

"I don't know."

"We've got to stop them."

"But we don't know for sure she's in it. Damn! Come on." She gave him a push to turn him back the way they had come. With Maggie leading, they raced back along the alley. Maggie prayed that neither of them would trip over something in the dark and go sprawling in the puddles, but apart from being splashed from head to toe, they made it safely back to Seymour and in a matter of minutes they were once again on Pender Street.

"Go get your car while I run along to Richards to see which way they turn when they come out of the alley," she panted.

"Okay," he rasped. "I'll be as quick as I can." But by the time he had opened the driver's door and flung himself inside, he could already see Maggie frantically waving to him from the intersection. Pushing the car into gear, tires squealing, he raced to where she was waiting, and in seconds she had yanked open the passenger door and thrown herself into the seat beside him.

"They turned up Richards," she gasped as he took off.

"Damn!" He had to brake suddenly to miss a drunk who was weaving slowly across the road in front of him. Fuming, he tapped his fingers on the steering wheel and wound down his window to shout, "Get a move on, for God's sake!"

The drunk stood in the middle of the road and cheerily waved his brown paper bag at him. "Wanna swig?" And he staggered over to Nat's open window.

"Get out of the road, you idiot," Nat yelled, recoiling from the fumes. "Oh, hell! Maggie," he said, peering round the corner, "there's no sign of them. We're too late."

"No, there they are," she shouted. "They've got a red light."

"Get out of the way," Nat roared at the drunk.

"If that's how you feel." The man drew himself up and walked ever so sedately to the curb.

"It's going to be tough trying to follow a brown van in the dark and the rain."

"You concentrate on driving and I'll keep an eye on them," replied Maggie. "But this proved difficult, as the van suddenly turned right onto Davie and into a stream of moviegoers and late diners. She thought several times that she had lost them as she peered through the rain-streaked windshield, only to catch another glimpse of the van under a streetlight ahead. "They're turning," she yelled suddenly.

"Which way?" He braked for a group who were slowly meandering across the road.

"Granville. They've turned left onto Granville."

"Where the hell are they going?"

Now Maggie had to really strain to keep them in sight, because although there was less traffic on this street, the lighting left a lot to be desired. "I think they're heading for the bridge."

"You're right, Maggie. I'll try and get a little closer." They were just six cars behind when they crossed the bridge and started up the South Granville hill. "They're turning left onto Sixteenth."

"Yes. I can see them." The van was only four cars ahead of them now. A few minutes later, he said, "They're signalling to turn right onto Oak."

After Nat had turned at Oak, Maggie suddenly said, "Of course! He said they were going to take her to 'the farm'! I bet they're heading for Richmond."

"I wish we knew for sure that she was in that . . . oh-oh, something's wrong up ahead." He leaned forward to peer through the wipers. "Lots of lights." By the time they reached Forty-first, the traffic had slowed down considerably. "Looks like an accident. Keep an eye on the van, Maggie."

They had to come to a complete stop at Forty-ninth, where two patrol cars with flashing lights and an ambulance blocked the intersection and police milled about in yellow slickers. In frustration, Maggie and Nat watched as the cars ahead of them, including the brown van, were let through one by one, but when it came to their turn, one of the cops suddenly stepped in front of the car and held up his hand to allow the ambulance to turn around for the journey back to the city. There was nothing they could do, and by the time they had crawled past the two-car crash site, their quarry was long gone. They drove on and over the bridge and into Richmond and then pulled off onto a side road. There was no point in going any farther.

"Bloody hell," Nat fumed. He couldn't hide his anger and frustration. He shut off the engine and turned to Maggie. "I think it's about time you explained why we were following a van that might or might not have Nancy in it."

So Maggie told him about the phone call from René, getting into the factory, having to hide for an hour behind the pile of boxes, seeing all the artifacts taken out of the crates, and then the arrival of the boss. "But I couldn't see who he was," she finished up. "We thought one of the men was coming over to our hiding place, so we crawled inside two crates, but I heard him telling Henry Smith to take Nancy to the farm." Her voice faltered.

"Maggie, why do you do this? I've told you over and over not to go off on these escapades without me."

"And where would we be if I had waited for you? And the thing is—what do we do about it now? I couldn't very well go to the police and say, 'Oh, by the way, I broke into Bakhash's warehouse and they are smuggling antiquities into the country and we think they've kidnapped Nat's ex-wife.' And anyway, they took the stuff away with them, so there's no evidence that any of it happened."

Nat turned the engine back on. "We're going back to your place and we *are going* to call George," he announced.

"There's only one thing, Nat . . ."

"And what's that?" he said angrily, ramming the car into gear.

"I'm absolutely starving."

He couldn't help laughing. "Oh, Maggie! You're priceless."

A half an hour later, they were sitting across from each other in Dan's Diner and digging into club sandwiches and fries, and Nat belatedly realized that he'd missed supper, too.

"So," Maggie said between bites, "dare I ask how your day in Victoria went?"

He quickly filled her in on his interview with Jake Houston. "The upshot is that if you agree that we go ahead with it, I'm to meet him and his staff tomorrow around noon."

"In Victoria?"

"No, no. They have an office in Vancouver. I gave it a lot of thought travelling back on the ferry, and I really think it will help us tie up the Dubois case—at least the murder angle."

"In what way?"

"Because Houston says that Dubois was definitely logging illegally, and he wants to know who his contacts were—especially those within his ministry."

"Do you think that's why he was killed?"

He shrugged. "I think it's our best hope of finding out." He signalled to the waitress for more coffee. "But I guess I should have been here with you, looking for Nancy instead of going to Victoria."

Maggie laughed. "I can just see you hiding behind a pile of cardboard boxes. But I think you're right; we'd better call George. And don't worry—she's definitely still alive, and we're going to find her." Reaching across the table, she placed her hand over his and gave it a squeeze. "Now take me back to where I parked my car, okay? I'm exhausted."

## CHAPTER FOURTEEN

It was still very early on Friday morning when Mrs. Mabel Maggs focused her small binoculars onto the place where the two men had been digging under the birdbath in her neighbour's back garden. She had been watching them since they arrived, and now the early morning light was slowly bringing all the trees and bushes into focus. Eventually one of the thugs—that was a good name for them, she thought—threw his shovel on the ground and kicked the pile of dirt in frustration. She was sure he was swearing. She watched them leave by the back alley but still waited a few minutes before letting the lace curtains of her back bedroom fall into place. Laying the opera glasses on the bureau, she left the room and, holding onto the banister for support, trod carefully down the stairs to her kitchen. "Time for my morning cup of tea."

DAYLIGHT BROUGHT MORE HEAVY rain. "It's Vancouver, so what else do you expect?" Maggie told Oscar as they skirted the puddles on the sidewalk. He gave her one of his doggy grins as he gently pulled her toward the park at the end of Fifth Avenue. "You don't care, do you, as long as you get your walk?"

As she dodged the dripping trees and the puddles, Maggie thought about her trip to Bakhash's factory with René, she and Nat chasing the dirty brown van, and George's impending visit. She could understand Nat being upset about her going to Bakhash's factory with René, especially since they still had no idea where Nancy was being held captive. The dratted woman had brought most of her problems on herself, but Maggie knew that they had to find her—preferably alive. She was still pondering the tricky situation when she arrived at the office an hour later and let herself in. There was no sign of Henny, but Nat's door was open and she could see he was on the phone.

"Henny called to say she won't be in until this afternoon," he called out as he put the phone down. "One of her boys is sick and she's arranged for a neighbour to pop in later to see how he is."

"I hope it's nothing serious."

"No. Just a cold. And the kid must be all of sixteen. But you know how Henny is about her family."

"Yes. I think our Henny runs her household like she does this office."

"You're going to Houston's Vancouver office today, aren't you?"

"Right after lunch. It'll be a good chance to get to know them and see whether it makes sense to take this on. I should be back by three at the latest. That sounds like George arriving now."

"So," George Sawasky said, eyeing the warm Danish pastries that Maggie had picked up from the local bakery, "perhaps you'd better start at the beginning."

"As long as you're not going to arrest me for breaking and entering," Maggie said as she passed the plate of Danish to him.

George laughed. "Maggie, if I arrested you for all the breaking and entering that I'm not supposed to know about, you'd be serving a very long stretch. Anyway, as I understand it from Nat, young René Dubois called you at home last night."

Maggie went through the whole story once again, finishing

up with her return home, hoping to grab a bite to eat before staking out Smith's emporium herself. "Luckily," she ended, "Nat called me."

"I'd been trying to get hold of her since shortly after six," Nat chimed in. "I was getting worried and was about to get in my car and drive to her place when she answered."

"And that's when the chase began," George said. "Are you sure that Nancy was in the van?"

Maggie glanced over to Nat. "That's the problem, George. We're not really sure. You see, Smith complained that he couldn't keep her at his emporium any longer, and that's when the boss man told him to take her to the farm."

"Did he mention a specific time?"

"No. Just that night."

"So when we saw the van leave," Nat said, "we were sure that she must be in it."

George reached for another pastry. "This is the same emporium where Nancy sold the bracelet, right?" he said before taking a large bite.

They both nodded.

"And you can't place the voice of this boss man?" he asked Maggie.

She shook her head. "I couldn't hear him properly from where we were."

Nat suddenly asked, "Have the West Van police got anywhere with Maurice Dubois's murder?"

"They'd love to pin it on one of that bunch at the fishing resort, but they can all provide alibis for each other. And they all say Dubois was there until the Saturday afternoon and then he simply disappeared, only to turn up dead on Hollyburn Mountain a couple of days later."

"And Jacquelyn's murder?" Maggie asked.

"Farthing says it was simply a robbery that went wrong. Someone knew she was alone and that she had valuable stuff. Unfortunately," George continued, "it's quite common to rob grieving spouses. Thieves find obituaries in the paper and follow up on them."

"Farthing could be right," Nat said. "After all, the theft of the antiquities did take place a couple of weeks before she was murdered." He sat deep in thought for a moment. "But I still think that the murders are connected."

"I agree with you. And now there's Nancy's kidnapping."

"I don't know if you realize it, George," Maggie said, "but the three I saw last night with that cache of Egyptian antiquities were all at that fishing resort over the New Year's holidays. And Mrs. Schaefer told me that both Edgeworthy and Smith were in North Africa with the 8th Army—so there is a connection."

"It's got to be some big-time smuggling racket," Nat said. "And Nancy's somehow got herself mixed up in it. I'm really worried for her, George."

"I know you are, Nat, but even if I got a search warrant for the Smiths' place, you can bet your bottom dollar Nancy won't be there." He stood up and reached for his coat. "In the meantime, you be careful," he said, and turning to Maggie, he added, "No more breaking and entering." He reached down from his six three height and gave Maggie a peck on the cheek. "Loved the pastries." He patted his stomach. "My wife won't let me have them."

IT WAS AFTER TWO when Maggie, deep in paperwork, heard the outer door opening. Stretching her arms over her head, she got out of her chair and made for the outer office, where Henny was hanging up her coat.

"Mr. Nat tell you my boy is sick?" Henny said. "My neighbour will go in and make sure he is okay." She dived a hand into her roomy tapestry bag, pulled out her new knitting project, laid it on her desk and then dived back into the bag for a large brown paper bag. "I have baked something different for Mr. Nat." She plonked a large round loaf next to her knitting. "Soda bread. My neighbour, Mrs. Reilly, showed me how."

"Soda bread! I haven't had that for years. My Irish grandmother used to bake it." She stopped suddenly. "Of course. It's Liam Mahaffy! The boss man is Liam Mahaffy and the farm they're talking about is Twin Maples—Mahaffy's stables." She turned and gave a very surprised Henny a hug. "Thank you."

"For soda bread?"

"For *Irish* soda bread." She reached up, grabbed both their coats from the bamboo stand and tossed Henny's over to her. "The Smiths' van wasn't going to Richmond. It was heading for the Deas Island Tunnel and Mahaffy's stables out in Delta! Come on! We're off to rescue Nancy."

"But what about Mr. Nat?"

"We'll leave him a note." Then she stopped. "But what about your boy?"

"It is only a cold he has. I call my neighbour and say I have to do some detecting." She popped the soda bread back into her bag and struggled into her coat while Maggie scribbled a note for Nat and left it on his desk.

Henny sat in the passenger seat of the Morris and clutched her large tapestry bag to her bosom as if it would protect her from the speed Maggie was driving. "Perhaps we get there safer if we go slow?"

"Sorry. My mind was on how to go about tackling Liam Mahaffy. I can't just bust in on him and ask if he's kidnapped Nancy."

"You will think of something when we get there," Henny answered. "You always do, Mrs. Maggie."

"Thanks for the vote of confidence." But her mind was still going over several scenarios for the confrontation ahead.

"YOU ARE SUCH a bad liar." Liam Mahaffy looked down at Nancy, trussed up and lying on an iron cot. "The Smiths dug under that damned birdbath and they didn't find a thing! I think it would be in your best interest to stop playing games and tell me what you really did with the stuff."

"I told you, Liam—I buried them in a bag right under that birdbath. They *must* be there!" She gave a little sob. "They couldn't have looked in the right place." Nancy was certainly not a brave person, and now she was hungry, thirsty and dirty, and her left cheek and eye were painfully swollen where one of Smith's sons had given her a few unnecessary vicious blows. "Take me home and I'll show you."

"My dear, it doesn't work like that. You tell us. We find the goods. Then if you're telling the truth . . ."

"I *am* telling you the truth. And how do I know you'll let me go?"

"You don't. We're willing to give you a few more hours to consider." He glanced at his Rolex. "Say midnight tonight." He gave a sardonic smile. "It's easier to get rid of a body after dark."

"Please, Liam, I'm so thirsty . . ." But he had already left the room, locking the door firmly behind him.

Nancy curled up in a fetal position and sobbed. *Why did I steal that junk? Nobody knows where I am, and nobody cares.* She was totally exhausted. A few minutes later, the door was reopened, and Mahaffy returned carrying a jug.

"I'm not totally unfeeling," he said, placing the jug on the night table. He pushed her roughly onto her side and untied the tight cords binding her wrists and ankles. "You won't be going anywhere. There's a toilet in there." And then he was gone.

Nancy listened to his footsteps getting fainter and fainter as he descended the stairs.

Struggling to sit up, she took a long drink of the water—it was wonderful—but it took several tries to get her numb legs working so that she could hobble to the toilet in the adjoining closet.

The bedroom she had been imprisoned in was obviously in an attic and was sparsely furnished with just the iron bedstead, a wooden chair and a rickety table. Before returning to sit on the bed, Nancy put the chair under the small window and gingerly climbed onto it to look outside. It told her little other than that the ground was a very long way down and the house was completely isolated. All she could see for miles were waterlogged fields with rows and rows of dead cabbage stalks and acres of rhubarb. There were no horse stables, paddocks or barns, or any sign of Liam's staff of workers that she had expected to see.

Climbing down from the chair, she sat on the side of the bed to think. "So where the hell am I?" She fell back onto the bed and stared up at the ceiling. "Even if Nat goes looking for me, he'll never find me here!"

"YOU WANT ME TO stay in car?" Henny asked nervously as a string of riders on huge horses, hooves clattering on the concrete driveway that fronted the complex of buildings, trotted past.

Maggie nodded. "I'll see if he's in his office before asking around."

She tapped on the office door and pushed it open. Liam Mahaffy was immediately on his feet and extending a hand to her.

"Well! It's Mrs. Spencer, the detective lady. What brings you to this neck of the woods? Don't mind the dogs—they won't hurt you," he added as his two German shepherds came over to sniff at her again.

He pointed to a chair. "Sit down and tell me what I can do for you."

"It's about Nancy ... Nancy Gladstone," she repeated when he responded with a blank look.

"Who the hell is Nancy Gladstone?"

"Didn't you meet her at that ski resort promotion lunch?"

"Oh! *That* Nancy. What about her?"

"She seems to have gone missing, and I wondered if you had seen her lately?"

He shook his head. "Haven't seen her since. You a friend of hers?"

"No."

The answer came out so curtly that Mahaffy raised an eyebrow and gave a little laugh. "Obviously not. So why the interest?"

"She's my boss's ex-wife."

"Oh! I see." He tried to hide his surprise before he continued, "Why isn't he doing the looking?"

"He is. We both are."

He got to his feet and walked around the side of the desk. "Sorry I can't be of any help, but I'm sure she'll turn up." And putting his hand under Maggie's elbow, he eased her out of the chair and over to the door. "At least let me see you to your car. You still driving that cute little red one?" The two dogs followed closely behind as he walked her to where the Morris was parked.

"Is that where you live?" Maggie asked, pointing to a sprawling rancher just beyond the stables.

"Oh yes. Have to be where the action is," he replied as she got behind the wheel. "Nice to see you've brought a bodyguard with you," Mahaffy added, nodding to Henny. Laughing, he closed her car door, turned and walked back to his office. Glancing in her rear-view mirror, Maggie could see that the two dogs watched the car until she reached the farm gate.

"What we do now?" Henny asked as they drove back down the lane.

"I don't think he could be keeping Nancy in the stables. There are too many people going in and out all day. So we need to get into his house." Maggie glanced at her watch. "It's nearly five. Do you need to get home right away, Henny?"

"Dirk will be home with the boys now," Henny said. Maggie knew that Henny's husband owned a garage and worked erratic hours, so it was lucky he'd have the time to spend with his two sons. Henny's next words confirmed Maggie's thoughts. "So it is okay for us to go on looking for Mr. Nat's old wife."

"That's great, Henny. Thanks. I'm going to double back and hide the car in that small side road near the stables. Then I'm afraid we'll have to wait until it gets dark before I can get back into the stables. This is the place," she added as she turned into a narrow side road and then drove her car under some evergreens. Turning off the engine, they settled down to wait.

Henny, diving once again into her copious bag, produced the soda bread and a knife. She handed a big wedge of bread over to Maggie, who would have given anything for a cup of hot tea to go with it, as it was rather dry, but she was grateful all the same.

Through the branches of the scrubby evergreens beside the car, they had a partial view of the road leading from the stables. Around six they watched several of Liam's workers leave, some on foot and others pedalling bikes. Even so, Maggie waited until a little after seven before finally opening her car door and very gingerly shaking the crumbs from her lap. The rain had stopped but the sky was still overcast, so hopefully she would be able to slip back to the stables unnoticed.

"If I'm not back in an hour, get to a phone and call Nat."

"We go together," Henny answered firmly, hauling herself out of the passenger seat. "But what about those big dogs?"

"Let's hope they're keeping the horses company."

IT WAS NEARLY FIVE thirty before Nat arrived back at the office. He was excited about the new case and couldn't wait to fill Maggie in, but there was no one in the office when he arrived, so he settled down at his desk, eager to make notes on his afternoon appointment.

He was so engrossed that a full hour had passed before he glanced up and saw Maggie's note propped up against his desk calendar. He knew immediately it meant trouble. "Oh, Maggie, what have you done this time?" He scanned the note, uttered several meaningful oaths, then thrust it angrily into his coat pocket.

He debated whether he should call George, but decided he needed more information before bringing him in. "Why the hell couldn't she have waited?" he asked himself.

Grabbing his keys, he returned to his car and headed out into the traffic.

MAHAFFY'S STABLES WERE AT least a hundred yards from the gate, but they were well lit. Maggie could see that at least four people were still working and moving in and out of the buildings. The house also showed a few lights, so she surmised that this was where she would find Mahaffy. Touching Henny's shoulder, she indicated that she was going to the right to follow the line of trees along the rail fence that bordered the property.

"Where are the dogs?" Henny asked nervously as she followed on Maggie's heels.

"In the stables . . . I hope," she whispered back.

Ten minutes later, Maggie stopped and indicated silently that she was going to cross the open space between the trees and the open garage where Mahaffy's silver Jag was parked. The office was located next to it, and light was filtering through its slatted blinds. "You stay here," she whispered, "while I take a peek through the office window." She kept her fingers crossed that someone wouldn't appear out of the dark and surprise her as she tiptoed past the garage to reach the office. But Liam Mahaffy was not in the room, and as far as she could tell, neither were the dogs.

*So where is he?*

Slipping back around the corner to the rear of the office, she saw that lights were streaming from windows at the back of Mahaffy's ranch-style bungalow and onto the garden beyond. She was about to head in that direction when a sudden touch on her shoulder made her whirl around in panic. It was Henny, still clutching her tapestry bag. Maggie, faint from fright, had to lean back against the wall until her heart stopped thudding before she could even think of taking another step. .

"I come too," Henny stage-whispered.

Indicating that she should stay close behind her, Maggie led the way down the side of the house and around the corner, where she took a quick peek through the closest window. It turned out to be the kitchen. Steam was rising from several pots on the stove. Through the partially open window, they could hear rock music blasting out of a small radio perched on the sill. An apron-clad man was whistling along with the music as he cleaned a long pine table. Ducking down, Maggie made a run for the other side of the window and turned back to signal for Henny to do the same, but had to stifle laughter as she watched her partner in crime inching her way over on all fours. It certainly didn't help the situation when the back door was flung open and a large tabby cat was pushed out into the night. The cat sat outside the closed door for a moment, preening its ruffled fur, then, seeing Henny on all fours, it walked over and rubbed its face all over hers. Pushing the loving feline away—it must have just finished a can of sardines—

Henny got to her feet with as much dignity as she could under the circumstances and briskly brushed herself down.

The next room appeared to be a dining room—the light was on and the table was set for one. All the rest of the rooms were in darkness, although one of them did have French doors leading out onto a patio, but they were firmly locked.

"We've got to locate Mahaffy," Maggie said. "You stay right here while I go back and take a look in the stables."

"But what about those big dogs?" Henny whispered back. "I should come with you."

"Stay here!" Maggie answered firmly.

"I hide behind those bushes." Henny pointed to a couple of rhododendrons on the edge of the patio.

"Just don't move." Maggie watched until Henny and the cat were safely out of sight before she ventured back toward the stables.

Keeping in the shadows as much as possible, Maggie made a wide approach to the outbuildings. She guessed it was feeding time, as the clattering of buckets and occasional snippets of conversation masked any slight noise that she might have made as she got closer. After about ten minutes, she was rewarded with the sight of Mahaffy and his leashed doggy companions. The two dogs immediately started sniffing the air, whimpering and straining in Maggie's direction, but Mahaffy jerked them back.

"Sit! I'm not letting you off to chase raccoons again."

Maggie breathed a prayer of thanks to whoever was watching over her as she turned and silently sped back to the house. She was still contemplating the problem of getting inside it when she peeked into the kitchen again and saw that the cook was on the phone: "Hi, boss. I'm off. The pie's in the oven. Needs another ten minutes or so, veggies in the warming drawer." He must have got an affirmative answer, because he then said, "See you in the morning."

Luckily, he didn't lock the kitchen door after his departure. Maggie waited only a few minutes to be sure that he wouldn't come back for something before she collected Henny from behind the bushes and led the way inside.

"We have to make this a quick search," she told her. "Mahaffy will be on his way home for dinner in a very short time." But she paused for a moment in the kitchen to take an appreciative sniff. "God! I'm hungry."

"I look in back rooms and you look in front ones," Henny ordered. Maggie couldn't help but smile as she obediently walked along a passage that led to three bedrooms. Nancy wasn't in any of them.

She had only just made it back to the kitchen and the back door when she heard two men talking—Mahaffy's northern Irish drawl and one other.

"Damn! It's Nat!" They were walking up the path from the stables and making for the back entrance. "Henny! Where are you?" she hissed.

"Getting pie out of oven," Henny answered, straightening up. "It is getting burnt."

"For God's sake, leave it!" But Maggie had to wait agonizing moments while Henny placed the pie on top of the stove before joining her outside. They made it behind the bushes just seconds before Mahaffy and Nat walked into the light.

"Do you always leave your place wide open?" Nat asked.

"No. And you can be sure I'll be having a few words with my cook about that," Mahaffy responded. "Now what do you want?"

"Maggie Spencer. Has she been here?"

"This afternoon. Looking for your ex-wife, I believe."

"About what time?" Nat insisted.

"Four-thirty or thereabouts. What's this all about, Southby? Why would I know where your ex-spouse is?"

"She's missing. And we're covering all the bases."

"Well, there's no reason for her to be here," Mahaffy snapped. "Now, if you'll excuse me, I have a business to attend to." He slammed the door shut.

"Didn't even offer me a beer," Nat muttered as he turned to go back.

"Psst! Nat."

"What the hell . . . !" An arm was waving at him from behind a bush. "What's going on?" he demanded once he had joined the two of them.

"She's not here," Maggie whispered, "so we've got to follow him. Come on." Stealthily she began to lead the way to the back of the garage.

"No." Nat grabbed her arm. "My car's out front. He's bound to be watching to make sure I leave."

"Okay. See you outside the gates." And touching Henny on the arm for her to follow, she led the way behind the garage and then sprinted for the trees.

Nat was right. As he walked around the house, he saw that Mahaffy had turned on the front porch light and was standing in the front entrance.

"I thought you'd got lost," he called out as Nat searched his pockets for his keys.

"You've got a big house to go around." Slipping into the driver's seat of the Chevy, he turned on the ignition and wound down the window. "Give me a call if Nancy should turn up."

"I've already told you—there's no reason for her to come here."

Maggie thought the man would never go back into the house, and when they eventually walked through the trees and out into the lane, they found Nat's car parked next to the Morris.

"Now what's going on?" he demanded.

Quickly, she explained how Henny's soda bread had given her the clue to Mahaffy's identity, and then deduced that the farm he had referred to was his boarding and riding stables. "But she's not here," she finished up. "Henny and I have already searched the place."

"And left the kitchen door wide open," he remonstrated, "If his cook insists he closed the door before he left, Mahaffy's sure to know that someone's been in his house."

"Not to mention the pie," she answered.

"Pie! What's pie got to do with anything?"

Maggie decided not to enlighten him. "Okay, we slipped up. But we've got to be ready to follow him when he comes out."

"What makes you think he's going to?"

"Stands to reason, if he's got Nancy."

"But Maggie, we don't know for sure that he has. And we could wait here all night." He put on his overhead light and peered at his watch. "It's already nearly eight."

Maggie leaned back on Nat's car while she thought. "Here's a suggestion," she said at last. "You take Henny home, and I'll wait here and get to a phone as soon as he's on the move."

"No, Maggie, it's the other way around. Nancy was my wife and I'll do the waiting. You take Henny home."

"But . . ."

"Just do what I ask . . . please."

Maggie could see that he was determined. "You promise to call me and let me know what's happening?"

"I promise. Just get going."

"THAT MAHAFFY MAN HAS lots of money." Henny broke the silence. Since leaving Nat behind, they had both been so tied up in their thoughts that they had travelled for miles along the dark country roads without saying a word.

"What makes you think that?"

"He has big stables and horses—that takes lots of money. He is a rich man . . ."

"It's probably all mortgaged to the hilt, Henny. I remember him saying that he'd started out with an old farm in Richmond . . ." She was silent for a moment. "Oh, my God, Henny! You've done it again."

"Yes?" Henny answered, puzzled.

"He said he still owns that farmhouse in Richmond. *That's* where they've stashed Nancy." She drove without speaking for another minute or so. "I just wish I could remember where he said it was . . ."

"Wood something," Henny said suddenly.

"How do you know that?"

"I type up your notes. No. 5 Road and another road that started with Wood."

"Henny," Maggie said glowing. "You are wonderful. I'll get you home and then see if I can find the place."

"No," Henny answered firmly. "Mr. Nat would never forgive me if you get hurt. I am coming too."

The overcast sky had partly cleared, and by the time Maggie's car emerged from the Deas Island Tunnel, the moon was casting ghostly shadows across the highway. But Maggie was too worried to appreciate the beauties of nature. She had been so sure that Mahaffy was holding Nancy at Twin Maples and she had been completely wrong. Now she was only too aware that she might be on another wild goose chase.

The traffic was light, and within minutes they were off the highway and onto No. 5 Road, passing rain-soaked farms that looked equally depressing in the wan moonlight.

"There's a turnoff coming up," Maggie announced, peering through the windshield. "But I can't see the street name in the dark." Pulling up at the corner, she climbed out of the car and was back inside within a minute. "This must be it, Henny. It's called Woodhead Road."

The narrow dirt road was bordered on both sides by deep, water-filled ditches, breached from time to time by plank bridges that led to sad-looking cottages squatting in sodden fields. Maggie drove slowly, keeping her eyes on the road. "Now all we've got to do is find the right house."

"That's it!" Henny announced, peering through the windshield. "See?" The dark shape of an old farmhouse sat forlornly in a muddy field.

Maggie stopped the car. "Maybe. But there's no light. I think I'll drive a bit further along and see if any of the other houses fit the description." But a few moments later, she was faced with a dead end. "I guess that must've been it," she said. "And now I've got to turn this thing around in the dark and not land us in one of those ditches."

"I get out," Henny volunteered.

"No. Just sit tight. One thing about these small cars," she added as she reversed, "is that they're great for getting out of tight spots." But it took her quite a bit of reversing and going forward before she got the car turned around. Henny heaved a great sigh of relief when they eventually pulled up outside the house again. Maggie got out of the car to have a better look. The house stood well back from the road and seemed to be clad in cedar shakes that had seen better days. "Doesn't look as if it's been occupied in years," she said.

"We go and see," Henny announced, clambering out of the car and knocking her tapestry bag into the road. Its contents went flying, and Maggie was sure she heard a muttered curse as her sleuthing partner gathered everything up, but as the words were Dutch, she couldn't be sure.

Together they gingerly crossed the ditch on the pair of wooden planks that had replaced the original bridge. The gate shrieked in protest as Maggie pushed it open, but there didn't seem to be a soul around to hear it. At this point the moon gave up playing hide-and-seek in the clouds and left them to find their way in total darkness.

"Wait," Henny whispered. A moment later, her enormous bag yielded a flashlight, and although it cast only a very faint beam, she played it over the house. All the windows facing the road were boarded up.

"We'll try the back," Maggie said, taking the flashlight from Henny and leading the way onto a muddy path that led around the side of the building past a sagging lean-to.

Suddenly, Henny grabbed her arm. "Someone's here," she said. She pointed to the path ahead.

Maggie shone the flashlight ahead of her and saw that there were footprints in the mud. "You're right." She crouched to look at them more closely. "They go both ways," she said. "Somebody came and went." Feeling their way carefully toward the backyard, they looked for signs of occupation—a light, anything. Nothing! Then Henny pointed out a tiny glimmer from a little window right under the point of the gable—a flickering candle, maybe?

NAT GOT OUT OF the car, stretched his arms over his head, glanced at his watch and leaned back against the hood of the car. "I'll give him another ten minutes," he muttered. While waiting, he had seen a couple of Mahaffy's workers arriving, probably for the night shift. But so far Liam Mahaffy himself was staying put. Nat's mind wandered from worrying about Nancy to wondering if they would ever find the double murderer, and then to the feasibility of taking on the logging scam job for the Forest Ministry. He was so engrossed that he almost missed the throaty sound of the guar's engine as Mahaffy's car came out of the gate and passed e end of the lane where Nat's car was hidden.

"Damn and blast!" Running around to the driver's side of the hevy, he jumped in, switched on the ignition and carefully nosed e car into the lane. *Got to stay well back. He's only got to see my adlights to know someone's following.* He watched the tail lights the Jag dimming in the far distance before he turned on his ihts and eased onto the road. A quick glance at the dashboard ck told him it was quarter to nine.

He felt a little worried when the silver car turned onto the ghway, as he knew he wouldn't have a chance of keeping Mahaffy sight if he opened up that powerful engine. "Where the hell's going?" Then it dawned on him. "He's going through the Deas land Tunnel. He's heading for the city!"

AGGIE STOOD WELL BACK in the wet grass and peered up at e attic window. "Definitely a light of some kind," she muttered. Ve've got to find a way in before Mahaffy turns up." But she was lking to herself, because her willing helper had disappeared up e back stairs.

"Door is locked," Henny commented when Maggie caught up ith her. "We will break the window glass?" But that was easier id than done, as the sash windows on the ground floor were ghtly closed and pieces of plywood had been nailed across each them.

"We need some kind of tool. What about that lean-to?" Using e flashlight, Maggie saw that it was half-filled with weathered ards, and on the wall were hung a few garden implements cluding a rusty axe. Several tins of nails came tumbling down as laggie felt along a plank shelf in the semi-darkness. "Drat." The o of them froze in their tracks and waited for a few minutes, it the eerie silence continued. Finally, Henny took the axe and

Maggie armed herself with a long-handled hoe. "Let's tackle that window by the back door," Maggie whispered.

They soon realized that the window was too high off the ground, and even Henny, who was at least six inches taller than Maggie, couldn't get a good enough swing with the axe to smash through the plywood.

"Give me the flashlight and you wait here, Mrs. Maggie, while I go look for something to stand on."

"We've got to hurry. Mahaffy's likely to turn up any minute." But she realized that she was talking to herself again as Henny had disappeared into the dark, and the only sound was lumber and implements tumbling to the ground. She was about to feel her way back to the lean-to when Henny reappeared empty-handed.

"You didn't find anything?"

Taking Maggie by the arm, Henny propelled her further along the back wall and around the corner, where she pointed the flashlight at a flight of stairs leading to a glassed-in porch. When Henny swung her axe at one of the porch windows, the noise seemed to vibrate all around them. Maggie quickly put her hand over Henny's to wait for repercussions, but the only thing they had disturbed was a dog further down the road. It took Maggie several minutes to remove enough glass with her gloved hand so that she could reach inside and unlatch the door.

"I haff the light," Henny said and led the way inside. But even though Maggie walked close behind Henny's bulk, she still got her fair share of cobwebs, and she became convinced that there were monster spiders clinging to her face and hair. Henny's light was now all but useless, and with their arms outstretched to feel their way, they stumbled over pails, bumped into a wringer washer and various other bits of furniture, boxes and heaven knows what. Finally Maggie, patting her way along the wall, located a light switch, and the single bulb hanging from the ceiling not only revealed the accumulated junk they had ploughed through but also showed them a glass-paned door that led into the main part of the house. Once again Henny wielded her axe.

NAT MADE SURE THAT he was well back from the silver Jag before they entered the tunnel, so it was just sheer luck that he noticed Liam Mahaffy's car veer off the freeway and onto the Steveston Highway exit. Nat followed the Jag in the distance until he saw it stop outside a corner convenience store. By the time Nat caught up, Mahaffy was outside the store in a telephone booth, talking animatedly on the phone.

Driving past the store, Nat eased into a spot further down the dark road to wait and watch in his rear-view mirror. Ten minutes went by before he saw Mahaffy hurrying back to his car. The Jag made a U-turn and headed back the way it had come. Nat waited a few minutes, made a U-turn with his lights off and followed the Jag. He was just in time to see the silver car turn back onto the highway, heading north once more.

The chase was on again!

AS MAGGIE REACHED FOR the light in the kitchen, she hoped that the shuttered window would do its job—but the choice was either to turn on the light or risk having an accident as they stumbled around in the dark. A door at the far side of the kitchen led to a hall and a staircase leading upward.

"We've got to make this quick," Maggie commanded as she bounded up the threadbare carpeted stairs. "If Nancy's here, then Mahaffy's not far behind."

Henny, still carrying her axe, gasped as she tried to keep up with her boss. It took several precious moments to peek in each of the four rooms on the second floor and then tear up the last flight leading to the attic. Maggie banged on the door. "Nancy?"

"I'm in here," Nancy yelled through the attic door. "But the door's locked."

"Of course it is," Maggie muttered, relief mixed with the inevitable irritation she felt towards Nat's ex-wife.

Henny marched purposefully toward the door with her axe. "Stand back," she yelled.

"Where's Nat?" was the first thing that Nancy demanded as the door crashed open.

Maggie looked at Nat's ex-wife and realized that it was a good thing the woman couldn't see herself in a mirror. Tears mixed with old mascara and dirt had streaked down her face, the usually beautifully coiffed blonde hair was tangled and the borrowed sweatsuit did little to enhance her figure. "He's out looking for you," she answered tersely. "Come on, let's get out of here. Lead the way, Henny."

The three of them raced down the stairs and back through the porch, with Maggie carefully extinguishing the lights one by one as they went. They flew across the plank bridge and Henny unceremoniously pushed Nancy into the back seat of the Morris before flinging herself in beside Maggie. Gunning the engine, Maggie drove down the dark road, turned onto No. 5 Road, and headed for the city.

EVENTUALLY, MAHAFFY TURNED OFF the freeway again onto Westminster Highway, negotiated a complicated series of turns to get onto No. 5 Road, and then within minutes made a right onto a narrow gravel road. Nat sensed they must be nearing the end of their journey. He pulled to the side of No. 5 Road just short of the intersection. Call it luck or intuition that made him wait a few minutes before following on foot, but as he went to open his door to step out, another car passed him and turned the corner. This time Nat climbed cautiously from his car and walked to the corner, grateful that there were no streetlights on this part of the island. Both cars were now parked with their lights on halfway down the narrow road, and Mahaffy and the other driver were standing beside them, talking. Then suddenly, the car lights went off, a flashlight came on, and Nat watched it bobbing off into the darkness.

He waited until the beam from the flashlight vanished, presumably behind a house, before venturing down the road. Just as he reached the two cars, the clouds parted and a shaft of moonlight showed him a plank bridge. He crossed it as quietly as possible, followed a muddy path and climbed the steps to the front door. Just his luck! It was boarded up, as were the windows on either side. By this time the moon had disappeared again, and he had to feel his way back down the stairs, cursing under his breath, and work his way toward the corner of the house. As he rounded the corner, he could see that there were lights on inside, and he was halfway up the stairs leading to a glassed-in porch when he heard the yells of rage coming from above.

"There's no way she could escape!"

"Didn't you tie her up?"

"No, but the door was locked, and . . ."

Nat didn't wait to hear any more. Grinning, he ran down the stairs and ducked into a tool shed he saw nearby. Moments later, Mahaffy and the other man came running out of the house, heading for their cars. Nat waited until all was quiet again before he emerged and in the utter blackness of the night made his way back around the side of the house and sprinted for the road. In his haste, he had forgotten that the plank bridge was narrow and slimy. The ditch he landed in was half full with muddy water from the recent rainstorm. The air was blue with his muttered curses as, soaking wet from his knees down, he had to haul himself out by clinging to the course clumps of weeds and grass that grew on the bank.

Half an hour later, Nat's car was parked outside Maggie's house and he was opening the front door with his key. Maggie and Nancy were seated at the kitchen table with drinks in front of them. Without a word, he picked up the bottle of cognac and poured himself a liberal drink.

"You're all wet," Maggie said, rising in alarm. Nat was sodden from the waist down.

"I fell in the bloody ditch," he said before knocking back half of his drink.

"You'd better go upstairs and change," Maggie commented. "You'll find your clean shirt in my closet. I'll put some hot coffee on."

"That's cosy," Nancy said, raising her eyebrows as she watched Nat ascend up the stairs.

On his return, Nat immediately pulled up a chair and turned to his very bedraggled ex-wife.

"Okay! Fill me in."

After their individual night's experiences had been discussed, Maggie asked the most important question. "What do we do now?" She glanced at the dishevelled Nancy. "I think you should take Nancy home so that she can get some clothes and her car."

"What if they're waiting for me there?" Nancy whimpered.

"There's a chance they won't think you'd go back to your own place," Maggie answered. "But you should go right away and get your stuff as quickly as you can. Have you a friend you can go to?"

"I could stay at your place, Nat."

"That's the first place those thugs will look," Maggie said, thinking that Nat was welcome to his ex-wife, but there was absolutely no way the woman was going to stay with her.

"What about that aunt of yours . . . the one who lives in New Westminster?" Nat asked.

"Aunt Marian? But it's too late to call her now."

"*Try*," Maggie snapped, pointing to the phone. "Tell her the power's off at your place or something."

Nancy reluctantly took the phone and dialed. The conversation was short, but the aunt agreed that her niece could stay until the power was restored. "She said that she was just about to go to bed," Nancy said as she replaced the receiver, "but she'd leave the door unlocked."

"Okay. So let's get going," Nat said, getting out of his chair.

"You can borrow one of my coats." Maggie reached into the hall closet and pulled out a grey wool coat with a hood. "Nat can bring it back later." She opened the front door and watched the two get into Nat's car and pull away from the curb.

Quickly rinsing the cups and glasses, she shooed Oscar and Emily out and waited apprehensively for them to return. After they were safely in again, she made sure that all the doors and windows were firmly locked before climbing the stairs to find comfort in her own warm bed. She hoped they made it before Mahaffy and friends decided to go back to Nancy's house to check. And then another thought came as she snuggled down.

*Should we have called George in on this?*

But she was beyond worrying anymore. She'd talk to Nat about that in the morning. She hoped that Henny had managed to think up a good excuse for being home so late, but she wasn't too worried, as Henny seemed to run the Vandermeer household, her husband Dirk, and her two sons exactly the same way as she did the agency office.

The telephone woke her. She turned on the light and checked the time. Two thirty. Nat's voice, a pleasant interruption to her dreams.

"Thought you'd like to know she is safely stowed with her aunt. See you in the morning and sweet dreams—if that's at all possible."

## CHAPTER FIFTEEN

It had forgotten to rain, and Maggie awoke to a bright, sunny Saturday morning. As she lay on her back and stretched her arms above her head, the previous night's adventures came rushing back to her. *Nat said there was another man at the farmhouse with Mahaffy and that he was the one doing the shouting. But he didn't recognize the man's voice. So that lets out Henry Smith with his Cockney accent. And the same goes for Bakhash. Could've been Edgeworthy, I suppose . . . but I can't see him as the head honcho.*

When the phone rang, she contemplated not answering it, but on the third ring, she gently pushed the sleeping Emily over to the other side of the bed and swung her feet to the floor. It was Nat to say that he'd filled George in on last night's episode and he wanted to meet with them in a couple of hour's time.

"Here?" Maggie asked, thinking that it would take more than an hour to tidy up her house for company.

"At the office."

"I'll be there as soon as possible."

"Okay. I'm going to call Henny and ask her to come in, too."

She pushed her rebellious thoughts away as she snuggled her feet into her slippers and walked downstairs to be greeted by Oscar. "I have to have my cuppa, Oscar, before I even think about a walk. Will the backyard do you?" What she really needed was a good hot shower and breakfast, she thought as she closed the back door on the dog. Her last meal had been a sandwich at her desk the day before.

NAT AND HENNY WERE waiting for her when she arrived at the office, and their Girl Friday didn't look any the worse for the previous night's activity. In fact, she was quite chirpy.

"Hope Dirk wasn't mad at me for keeping you out so late?" Maggie asked, peeling off her coat.

"He was worried, but I told him you needed me."

"And Pieter? Is he any better?"

"Ja! It is a bad cold. His brother, Bartel, has it now." She marched toward Nat's office, carrying two cups of coffee. "Mr. Nat ask me to bring your coffee in his office."

"I hope I have time to drink it before George gets here," Maggie said, taking one of the cups from Henny. But she had only taken a sip when the outer door opened and George arrived, accompanied by a tall, blond, moustached man. "So you've been up to your usual hijinks, have you, Henny?" he greeted her.

Maggie was amused to see Henny blush when George put his arm around her shoulders. "I've told my friend here all about your famous cookies." He continued into Nat's office and bent to give Maggie a hug. "Maggie, I'd like you to meet Quentin De Meyer."

Maggie extended her hand to the familiar-looking man. His blue eyes twinkled as he gave her a slight bow.

"Pleasure to meet you, Mrs. Spencer."

*Where have I met him before?*

"Hi, Nat," George said. "I hope you don't mind, but I've asked Quentin to sit in."

Nat, looking puzzled, reached across his desk to take the man's hand in his. "No. That's fine."

"Shall I bring coffee?" Henny asked.

"That would be great, Henny," George answered.

"So what's this all about?" Nat asked once they were all seated.

"Before I tell you, I want you and Maggie to fill us in on Nancy's abduction."

"And, before I tell you anything," Nat said, turning to the other man sitting quietly by, "I want to know what your interest is in all of this, Mr. De Meyer?"

"Special Agent De Meyer," George answered for him. "Quentin is with Interpol, and he's been chasing an antiquities smuggling ring between Cairo and Vancouver."

"Aha!" Nat said, and he and Maggie exchanged looks.

"So if you wouldn't mind," George prompted.

So Maggie explained, but just when she got to the part about breaking into the farmhouse in Richmond, Henny returned with coffee for George and Quentin, and interrupted Maggie's story with, "I break the window glass." She placed the cups in front of the two men and added with relish, "With an axe."

Nat then explained how he had gone to look for Maggie at Twin Maples and his subsequent tailing of Mahaffy's car.

"And you say you didn't recognize the other man with Mahaffy?" George asked.

"I didn't hang around long enough to get a close look at him. After I realized that Maggie had been there before me and helped Nancy fly the coop, I got out before they discovered me."

"We think the smuggling started during the war," De Meyers started to explain. "We're sure that Mahaffy and Bakhash are in it, but we've yet to find the head of the ring. And catching them in the act is also paramount. That's why we'll need to keep Mrs. Southby's kidnapping quiet for a while."

"She calls herself Mrs. Gladstone—it's her maiden name," Nat said quietly.

"I take it that she somehow came into possession of some of Dubois's Egyptian jewellery?"

"She insists it was a gift."

"You said that Nancy is with her aunt?" George asked.

"In New Westminster."

"I think we should get her into a safe house until this is over."

"That would certainly relieve my mind," Nat said.

"She's had a very bad scare," Maggie chimed in. "She was sure that Mahaffy was going to kill her." Suddenly, she turned to George's companion. "Where have I seen you before?"

"Yes," Nat said, "I know I've seen you before, too."

"The day you were in Arnold Schaefer's office," Quentin replied.

"Of course," Maggie said. "You were waiting to have an interview with him. What happened to his previous employee?"

"We made sure he was suddenly offered employment elsewhere—with twice the pay—so Schaefer was desperate."

"And you just happened to turn up with the right credentials," Maggie replied.

"I can count on your discretion?"

"That's part of our business," Nat answered. "Discretion." He was thoughtful for a moment. "You know, I've suddenly realized who the other man was at the farmhouse." They all looked at him expectantly. "It was Schaefer!"

"That's why I wanted the job there," De Meyer said. "We thought he might be the brains behind this ring."

"At least we know where they'll all be next weekend," George said as he stood to shrug into his overcoat.

"Where?" Nat asked.

"Quentin overheard Schaefer on the telephone. He's arranged a getaway weekend at the same fishing lodge."

"You mean St. Clare's Cove?" Maggie asked, surprised.

"He was very insistent that they all attend and bring their wives so it will look innocent—he stressed that it was a very important matter."

"Oh! How I would love to be a fly on that wall," Nat said.

IT WAS NEARLY ELEVEN thirty when Nat received a phone call from George. "Mission accomplished," he said. "Nancy made a bit of fuss, but when we pointed out that her life was in danger, she agreed to the safe house."

"I wonder what happened to that jewellery?" Maggie mused after Nat told her of George's call. "Nancy insisted that she buried it in her back garden and I believe her. But she says that Mahaffy was equally insistent that his men dug where she told them, and it wasn't there."

"She's not going to be safe until that stuff's found," Nat answered. "By the way, I hope it's all right with you, but I've made reservations for us for next weekend, too."

"How lovely! Where are we going?"

"The St. Clare Resort. We're catching the Friday afternoon sailing from Horseshoe Bay to the Sunshine Coast."

"But that's like walking into the lion's den," she exclaimed. "What are they going to say when we turn up?"

"Not much they can say, is there? They don't own the place."

"Well, I know you said you'd love to be a fly on the wall when that lot gets together, but . . ."

"And this is almost as good. Come on, I'm taking you and Henny out for an early lunch."

THE FOLLOWING WEEK WAS a quiet one for the Southby and Spencer Agency, and by Wednesday morning Nat was back in the Vancouver office of the Forests Ministry. Jake Houston, true to his word, had found a small cubbyhole for him to work in, and Nat was soon immersed in the masses of files and papers that had been piled onto a battered wooden desk. The only window overlooked part of English Bay, and at first he found it hard to concentrate when the weather was so lovely and he could see sailboats dotting the water between freighters lying at anchor, waiting for berths at the grain terminals. But after a while, he forgot the view and immersed himself in reading the many memos, letters and other documents, and it didn't take him long to see how easy it was for unauthorized logging to go on unnoticed in remote parts of British Columbia. He began making notes.

At noon on Friday, Henny was still at her desk typing as Nat and Maggie prepared to leave for their weekend at the resort. "C'mon, Henny, time to go home!" Nat said.

"I will just finish this report, Mr. Nat, then I start Monday with a clean desk," she said, waving them out the door. "I will lock up the office. Don't you worry."

Fifteen minutes later, she was just covering her typewriter when the office door opened and René Dubois entered.

"Is Mrs. Spencer in?"

"You have just missed her. She and Mr. Nat are gone away for the weekend."

"Oh." René sat down, looking despondent. "She told me to report if anything happened at Bakhash's factory."

Henny uncovered her typewriter again and rolled a sheet of paper into it. "And you have something to report?"

"I wanted to tell her that my boss is sure one of the staff touched his crates."

Henny typed this information and then looked up expectantly. "So people are not happy with him . . ."

"Especially the men who usually unload the crates. One of

hem asked Bakhash if he was accusing him of stealing. He sorta
backed down after that. So where has Mrs. Spencer gone?"

Henny didn't look up from her typing. "To that fishing
lodge."

"You mean St. Clair Cove? What's she doing there?"

"She is detecting," Henny said.

"But that's where Bakhash has gone, too," René said slowly.
What's going on up there?"

Suddenly, Henny remembered Maggie's many admonitions
about giving out information, and she was desperately trying
to figure out how to take back what she had already said when
the phone rang. "Southby and Spencer Agency. Henny speaking . . . Oh, it is you, Mr. George . . . No, they are gone for the
weekend . . . What is that? . . . Oh dear! When did she . . . ?" She
listened for a while and then said, "I'll be sure to tell them if they
call. Mr. Nat will be very upset . . . Oh, I hope it is not that . . ."
After saying goodbye, she replaced the receiver and sat staring at
it worriedly.

"Has something happened to Mrs. Spencer?"

"It is Mr. Nat's old wife that is in trouble. Mr. George thinks
the kidnappers have kidnapped her again . . ."

"Kidnappers?" René asked.

And once more Henny momentarily forgot Maggie's admonitions. "Mr. Nat says it is all because she took that jewellery . . ."
Then, realizing she had once more said too much, she quickly
rose from her chair and rolled the sheet of paper from her typewriter. "I tell Mrs. Maggie you called, okay?"

# CHAPTER SIXTEEN

They hadn't been on the Blackball ferry since the previous September, when they had to go to Gibsons to break the news to Johanna Evans's parents that she had been brutally murdered. Maggie wondered how they were coping and if they had managed to put their lives back together. She shuddered as she leaned over the railing and watched the water flowing past, knowing that she would have been absolutely devastated if it had been one of her daughters. Nat, standing beside her, put his arm around her shoulders and drew her to him.

"I know exactly where your thoughts are, Maggie," he said quietly, "but unfortunately in this business we do come up against the seamier side of life. Take a deep breath of this wonderful sea air and admire those magnificent mountains. See, there's still a lot of snow on them."

He was right. The view was just as spectacular as their last trip to the Sunshine Coast, and unlike many commuters who used the ferry on a regular basis, Maggie wished the trip would last longer than the usual hour. But all too soon the boat was bumping its way into the slip and the passengers were back in their cars and waiting to disembark.

THE IRON-SPIKED GATES OF the resort were open when they

arrived, and they were soon driving down a long tree-lined gravel lane that led to a parking lot on the landward side of the main building. Nat parked the car right next to a woodshed piled high with cordwood. The lodge and the cabins they could see through the trees were, as Stella had commented, definitely rustic and rather run-down.

Nat pinged the bell at the reception desk while Maggie and Oscar waited patiently beside the luggage. "Nat Southby. We have a reservation," Nat said when the desk clerk appeared from her small office behind the desk.

"Mr. and Mrs. Southby. How nice to meet you," she said, reaching for a key on the board behind her. "We've put you in a lovely double room overlooking the cove," she continued. "Would you please sign here?"

As Nat signed the register, Maggie couldn't help her feeling of discomfort. What would her mother say if she saw them posing as husband and wife? Or her grandmother, Maggie thought, God rest her soul. Maggie felt ridiculous as she felt the crimson stain her cheeks, but she just couldn't feel completely comfortable and adult about the whole thing. She wasn't a film star or a teenager or someone else who could take such a thing lightly. She diverted herself by thinking about Oscar. She was equally worried that he wouldn't be welcome. However, Oscar did his bit to seem angelic by wagging his tail and giving the receptionist one of his doggy grins. That settled it.

The corner room they were shown to was large and airy, though badly in need of redecorating. But the receptionist was right—it did have a splendid view of the beautiful little cove, as well as a second window that overlooked some cabins in the forested area to the north. It took them only a few minutes to freshen up and set out to explore before dinner. There was a grassy area—it couldn't be called a lawn—that led down to a stony, shell-encrusted beach and a floating wooden walkway, where boats of all sizes bobbed up and down at their berths. By now the sun was low in the sky and it cast a golden path over the shimmering water, where screeching gulls dipped and cormorants dived to look for their supper.

Maggie gave a long sigh of contentment. "This is absolute heaven." She turned and gazed back at the old lodge. A covered wooden veranda stretched from one end of the building to the other, with three wooden steps leading from the crushed oyster-shell pathway to the open centre of the structure. Rattan chairs, tables and a couple of rocking chairs had been set on either side of a doorway that Maggie realized led directly into the rear of the lodge. To its left were the three small cabins they had seen from their room, nestled among cedars and arbutus under a stark, almost bare granite bluff. To its right stood half a dozen larger cabins, each with a private path through the trees to the beach. Raising her eyes to the land that rose sharply above the main building, Maggie could see three more cabins partially hidden by trees and undergrowth, and she pointed them out to Nat. "They must be on that side road that turned off to our left just after we came through the gate."

"But who'd want to stay in one of those?" he said. "You'd only get a squint at the ocean from there."

"I wonder if any of the motley crew have arrived," Maggie said.

"I didn't see any of them on the ferry," Nat answered.

"Well, we'll know at dinner, I guess."

"Come on then, I'm starved. Let's go!"

Their table for two, which was set in an alcove beside a large uncurtained window, also overlooked the cove. Maggie ordered poached salmon and Nat a large, rare steak. While they waited for the meal to arrive, she sipped on a glass of white wine while Nat, as usual, had a beer. The food was worth the wait, as both the salmon

d steak were excellent. After their plates had been taken away,
Maggie sat back in her chair and contemplated the dessert menu.
"Crème brûlé sounds delightful."

"Hello!" Stella Edgeworthy stood looking incredulously
own at them. "I couldn't believe my eyes when I saw you two.
What on earth are you doing here?"

"You told Maggie how picturesque the area was," Nat
answered as he neatly folded his table napkin, "so we decided to
steal a weekend away. But what a surprise to see you here, too.
Are you on your own?"

"No. Robert is over there." She pointed to a table on the other
side of the room. "And Arnold Schaefer is here, too," she added.
"We've got adjoining cabins." She indicated the cabins to the right
of the lodge.

"Surprised we didn't see you on the ferry," Maggie said, waving
an obviously displeased Robert Edgeworthy. "But I noticed
that most of the passengers stay in their cars, anyway."

"We only got here about half an hour ago," Stella explained.
She looked over to where her husband was beckoning to her.
"Must go. Arnold has arrived."

Maggie turned and gave another wave to Schaefer as Stella
departed.

"And now they know we're here," Nat said, grinning. He beck-
ned to the waiter.

"Two coffees and a crème brûlé for the lady."

The moon had risen by the time they finished eating, and
where earlier there had been a path of gold across the water,
the cove now shimmered in ghostly silver. The temperature had
dropped, and Maggie shivered as she stood in front of the bedroom window and gazed across at a small island that was showing
pinpricks of light. "That could almost be the island where I was
imprisoned."

Nat slid his arms around her. "It seems a long time ago," he said. "Your very first case with the agency." He turned her around to face the bed and Oscar, who was thumping his tail on his blanket. "Why don't you get ready for bed and I'll take our friend Oscar here for his walk."

Maggie reached up to give Nat a kiss. "You're a very nice man, Mr. Southby."

"I WONDER IF THEY'RE all here now?" Maggie leaned across the breakfast table to pour Nat some more coffee from the carafe the waiter had left for them. "Stella's bound to have warned them of our arrival."

Nat grinned. "And they are now speculating on *why* we're here. I think our first task is to find out where each of them is staying."

"Well, we know that the Edgeworthys and Arnold Schaefer are in the big cabins by the water, so it shouldn't take much work to find the others." She poured coffee for herself. "I guess it will mean another long walk for Oscar." She looked at her watch. "Let's give them a bit of time to be up and about. Of course," she added, "we could just ask at the desk."

As it happened, they didn't have to do either, because Stella appeared again as they were about to get up from the table.

"You certainly surprised a lot of people by turning up here last night," she greeted them.

"Are there more of your crowd here besides Mr. Schaefer?" Nat asked as he signed the chit.

"I thought there was only going to be him and us, but everyone else that was here at New Year's has come, too." She gave a shudder. "I think it's kinda of ghoulish. I certainly wasn't that keen on coming back . . ." She stopped, realizing that perhaps she was saying too much.

"Are you all staying in the cabins?" Maggie asked.

"The Smiths are next to Arnold, and the Bakhashes are in the next one with the Grossos." She paused to look abstractedly out of the window. "Their wives are sisters, you know."

"So we understand," Nat answered. "Liam Mahaffy was here at New Year's, too, wasn't he?"

"Yes. He's driving up later this afternoon." She turned toward the dining room door. "Better be off. Just came over to the dining room get some coffee for breakfast." She waved the carafe she was holding and was gone.

"You may not agree with me, Nat," Maggie said later as they were getting ready for their walk with Oscar, "but she's either a good actress or she really doesn't know what's going on with that crowd." She bent to clip on Oscar's leash, then picked up the small area map she'd discovered in their room. "Let's go and explore this little lake. It's called Hotel Lake, for some reason."

"Perhaps there's a hotel on it."

"I hope those clouds don't mean rain," Maggie commented as they started up the steep driveway that led to the road above the resort. There was no hotel at the lake—only a small cabin—and from there they walked down the hill to Irving's Landing. They had barely made it back to the lake before the rain started in earnest and they had to hightail it back to the resort.

"Shame we didn't have time to hike up that hill overlooking the lake," Nat commented with a grin as they changed from their wet clothes.

"You mean you're *glad* we didn't have time to explore it," she answered as she began towelling her wet hair. "Hills aren't your thing."

Lunch was ready when they descended to the dining room, and they were soon seated at their table and eating bowls of a wonderful seafood chowder.

"This is the life," Maggie breathed as she took another heavenly spoonful. She looked up suddenly. "That sounds like a floatplane coming in." She peered through the rain. "I wouldn't fancy flying in this weather."

Nat laughed. "The weather has to be really bad to stop those pilots."

They watched the plane circle the small cove before gently touching down and taxiing to the end of the dock. A few minutes later, a bundled-up, suitcase-laden figure emerged and began to stagger up the floating walkway that bobbed up and down in the swell. Once on stable land, the man made a beeline for the covered-in veranda.

"Another guest?" Maggie asked the waiter as he removed their plates.

"No, that's our Mr. Gunter," he said, and then in response to her inquiring look, he added, "One of the owners."

"We'll take our coffee in the lounge," Nat said as they rose from their table.

"Very good, sir. There's a nice fire going in there. Good afternoon, Mr. Gunter," he said, turning to the late arrival entering the dining room.

"Afternoon, Joe. Weather's sure turning nasty." Gunter looked around the room. "Bring me some hot soup and coffee at Mr. Edgeworthy's table."

Nat, holding the door open for Maggie, managed a quick glance to where Gunter was greeting Robert Edgeworthy. "What's the betting he's going to try to get Edgeworthy's Real Estate to take over from Maurice Dubois to sell the lots?" he whispered to Maggie.

"Could be."

THE LOUNGE HELD AN assortment of cretonne-covered sofas and armchairs that had seen better days. An old piano stood against one wall, and a row of French doors, half covered by faded red velvet curtains, opened out onto the veranda. Maggie led the way to the sofa that was closest to the cheery fire.

"Thank you," she said as the waiter placed coffee on a rattan coffee table. She waited until he had gone before turning and saluting Nat with her cup. "It's going to be very hard going back to cooking my own meals." She sighed and stretched her legs towards the blaze.

"Did you see the note taped to the door as we came in?" Nat asked.

"Something about the lounge being closed this evening for a private party. What do you bet that it's the motley crew getting together?"

Nat shrugged. "No bets. There's only another dozen or so people here, apart from us."

"And Stella did say that Mahaffy is driving up sometime this afternoon."

Nat walked over to the French doors and peered out. "Do you think if I hid out there tonight, I'd hear what's going on?"

"No," she answered. "The glass in French doors is too thick, and I don't think that gang would oblige you by leaving them open in this weather." She picked up a magazine and idly leafed through the pages.

He settled behind a discarded newspaper. "Let's see what's going on in the world." Then he looked at Maggie over the top of the paper. "Our room's right above," he said, nodding upward. Then he grinned. "Maybe there's a convenient heat register where we would be able to hear."

Maggie shook her head, laughing. "That only happens in the movies."

Nat soon abandoned the newspaper to walk over to the French doors again. The wind had gathered a lot more strength and was now ricocheting off the granite bluff and hitting the north side of the lodge so that the old building seemed to shudder.

"Glad we're in the warm," Maggie observed, placing her magazine back on the coffee table. "There's a pack of cards over there. Fancy getting beaten in a game of Gin?"

Nat beat her five to two.

AS THE DAY PROGRESSED, the storm worsened, and around four o'clock the power went off. The high winds had knocked down both power and telephone lines, one of the staff informed the guests with barely disguised glee, and he added the information that several fallen trees had also blocked the main road. "I guess you're all stranded here," he said.

Luckily, the lodge used propane gas for most of the heating and cooking, so dinner went ahead as scheduled, and the candles placed on each table gave a romantic atmosphere to the dining room. There was even a certain cosy feeling about being cut off from the outside world, and after lingering for a while over their coffee, they picked up the candles from their table to light their way back to their room.

"THEY'VE BEEN DOWN THERE talking for a least a half-hour," Nat fumed later as he bent to read his watch by one of the flickering candles. "We're missing anything useful they may be saying!"

The candles spluttered and wavered as he paced up and down the room. "There's got to be some way to find out what's going on." He grabbed his raincoat from the closet and headed for the door. "I'm going down the back stairs and around to that veranda." And he was gone.

Maggie waited fifteen minutes for him to return, and then she, too, reached for her raincoat. When Oscar followed her to the door, she grabbed his leash and clipped it to his collar.

"You're not going out in this storm?" the receptionist asked surprise.

"My dog doesn't understand weather," Maggie replied, indicting Oscar, who, with his usual doggy grin, was eagerly pulling r toward the main door.

"No, Oscar," she said, "we'll take the back way." She turned the receptionist. "At least I can dash back to the shelter of the randa if it gets too bad."

"If I were you," the girl answered, "I'd stay under the shelter d just let him run off and do his thing."

"Good idea. Come on, Oscar, this way," and she led him down e narrow corridor to the entrance on the waterfront side of the dge. She eventually won the tug-of-war with the wind and man-ed to open the door onto the veranda. "Nat!" she called softly. it apart from the old wicker armchairs and rockers, the deck is completely empty. She bent and unclipped Oscar's leash. Jow don't wander off too far," she admonished before she left e veranda to check around the far side of the lodge. When she ard Oscar barking back on the waterside of the veranda, she rned and ran back the way she had come. But just as she passed e last of the bank of French doors, it was opened outward with ch force that she was sure all the occupants in the room heard r gasp in surprise.

"What the hell did ya open that blasted door for?" someone lled from inside the room.

"I cannot breathe with all this smoke!" Maggie realized by the cent that it must have been one of the Egyptian sisters who had ened the door.

Maggie allowed her thumping heart to quieten before she ked taking her flashlight out of her pocket and going to the far d of the veranda, where she could lean out over the rail. "Oscar! scar!" she called, sweeping the small beam up and down. When there was no sign of him, she turned back. "Oh, no!" She froze in her tracks. The dog was standing in the doorway to the lounge. "Oscar, come here." The whispered order was blown away by the wind. "Oscar!" she called louder.

The dog, totally unaware of Maggie, poked his nose between the billowing velvet curtains covering the doorway. Then, before Maggie could take a step closer to grab him, Oscar, his tail still wagging furiously, pushed all the way into the room.

"Get that bloody dog out of here!" Schaefer yelled.

"It belongs to that Spencer woman," Rosie Smith shouted. "Git! Go on, you nasty thing, git!"

Maggie raced back to the corner of the building. "Oscar! Oscar!" she called out toward the water as loud as she could. "Oscar! Where are you?"

She heard him give a yelp before he came hurtling out onto the veranda. He was followed by Henry Smith, who peered right and left into the darkness before spotting Maggie.

"I'm so sorry," she said, grabbing hold of Oscar's collar. "He got away from me."

"Keep yer mutt on his bleeding leash," he snarled before returning to the room and slamming the door shut.

"The same to you," she muttered, bending to attach the leash. "Now see what you've done, Oscar? I won't be able to hear what they're saying."

"What the hell's going on?" The beam from Nat's flashlight played over her as she straightened.

"And where the hell have you been?" she shot back.

"Snooping around the cabins while everyone's fully occupied in there."

"In this weather?"

"Yeah! It was a wasted effort. So what's going on?"

"I'm going to take Oscar back to our room," she told him.

"I'll be back in a minute." She returned through the rear door, gave a cheery wave to the young woman manning the desk and ascended the main stairs. Her return trip was via the back stairs. She found Nat standing near the French doors, one of which was again slightly ajar.

"What's going on?" she whispered, sidling up to him.

"Shh," he whispered back. "One of the Egyptian women opened the door."

"I'm not so sure you weren't the one what offed him." It was Rosie Smith's grating voice. "After all, you . . ."

"She's got a point, Arnold," Robert Edgeworthy cut in. "You came back from fishing before the rest of us did."

"I can assure you," Schaefer replied icily, "although I'm glad that son of a bitch is dead, I didn't do it. And that means one of you did."

For a long minute, there was only the general rumble of indignant voices, then they heard, "What about you, Jerry? You've got the most to lose of any of us."

Maggie decided that it was Robert Edgeworthy asking the question.

"It wasn't *me* he was blackmailing," Bakhash answered testily. "I only import the stuff."

"And I repeat," Schaefer snarled, "I did not kill either Maurice or his stupid wife, but one of you did, and that's endangering the whole operation!"

"So which one of you beauties did the honours?" It was Liam Mahaffy's Irish brogue.

"You haven't so much to be proud of yourself, Mr. Mahaffy," Bakhash growled. "You let that woman get away with all that stuff we took back from Dubois."

"Which she would never have got her hands on at all if Robert hadn't left it lying around his office!" Mahaffy countered.

"How was I to know she'd get into my file room?"

"Ah! But I have remedied that situation." Mahaffy chuckled. "I have re-rescued her from the place where the police stashed her."

"When did you manage to do that?" Bakhash asked.

"Last night. And the Smith boys are taking great care of her as we speak."

Nat's hand tightened on Maggie's arm. Nancy was in trouble again! Just then a strong gust of wind picked up the velvet curtain and sent it flying horizontally into the room.

"Shut the door!" Henry Smith yelled. "That wind's blowing out the bleeding candles!"

Maggie and Nat slid further along the wall before the door was slammed shut once again.

"Come on," Nat said, putting his arm around Maggie's shoulders. "Let's go."

# CHAPTER SEVENTEEN

Sergeant George Sawasky and Special Agent Quentin De Meyer waited impatiently for the ferry to dock.

"We should have been here yesterday," De Meyer fretted, "and by air, not this damned boat."

"There was no way a float plane would have flown in that weather," George answered irritably. "And this morning all the choppers were out looking for survivors from those two missing fishboats. Anyway," he added, "the road was only re-opened this morning, so that gang up in Pender weren't going anywhere."

"Did you manage to contact your friend Southby?"

"No," George answered. "But I think I know where that bugger and his sidekick are," he added darkly. His police radio suddenly crackled. "Come in," George said as he grabbed the microphone.

"Coast Guard leaving Vancouver with Customs and Excise officers on board. ETA 1300 hours."

"Roger. Out."

"Will we make it in time?" Quentin asked anxiously.

George glanced at the clock on the dashboard before answering. "Yes. We've got just under two hours to get up there."

NANCY COULDN'T BELIEVE THAT Liam Mahaffy had found her again. Her only consolation was that at least this time she was fully dressed, although the thugs had taped her mouth and tied her feet and hands.

So much for police protection, she told herself. The cops had obviously bungled the whole thing, and Mahaffy had followed her right from her aunt's house.

By the look of the rustic walls and furnishings, she knew that she was now in a very small cabin, and by the sound of the wind and waves, she could tell she was close to the sea. Tears of self-pity slid across her face and soaked the thin pillow of the cot on which she was lying. She must have been drugged, as she had very little memory of the journey. I never did like that Sawasky, she thought. He just led that rat Mahaffy straight to me.

Her mind went back to her arrival at the safe house. At last she had been able to wear her own clothes and, more importantly, have her own makeup kit. And although the safe house apartment had been very small, she would have been able to accept it for a few days if the know-it-all policewoman who was assigned to protect her had not absolutely refused to go to a drugstore and get Nancy a bottle of nail polish remover—even though Nancy's nails had been completely ruined trying to claw her way out of that farmhouse. But Constable Marybeth Peckworth told her she had to wait until it was safe for her to return home. Of course, there was nothing else Nancy could do but slip out while the woman had her nose in one of her eternal paperbacks. Unfortunately, that had been her undoing. Mahaffy and his henchmen had been waiting for her outside the building.

She moved restlessly, trying to get herself into a more comfortable position. I've been here hours, she thought. I've got to stand up. She wriggled to the side of the bed and twisted her body around so that she could dangle her bound legs over the edge. Then she took a deep breath and squirmed until her feet finally met the floor. It took her several attempts to stand upright

d then she had to wait a few more moments for the giddiness to
bside before she could hip-hop over to the small half-curtained
indow. Bending her neck, she slid her head under the curtain.
he faint early morning light silhouetted ghostly trees, bushes and
e masts of moored yachts. She realized that the weird tinkling
unds were coming from the yachts' rigging that was swinging
the sharp breeze. She gave a shuddering sigh. At that moment
e would have even welcomed being rescued again by that bitch
aggie.

HE HIGH WINDS AND rain had died during the night, leav-
g fresh piles of logs and branches marooned on the shore. A
atery sun was doing its best to filter through the low clouds, and
agulls and ragged crows shrieked and fought as they foraged for
od in the mounds of seaweed. But the dining room was warm
d cheerful from the log fire burning in the huge grate.

"Thank goodness the kitchen runs on gas," Nat said, dipping
piece of bread into the golden yoke of his egg. "But I guess they
n't make toast."

"How can you eat breakfast at a time like this?" Maggie asked.
We've got to let the police know that Nancy's been kidnapped
ain."

"Me not eating breakfast isn't going to find Nancy any quicker,"
answered, "and as to the cops . . ." he beckoned the waitress over.
Have they repaired the phone lines yet?" he asked her.

"They were still dead a few minutes ago," she answered. "We'll
t you know as soon as they've been fixed."

"At least this old building survived," Maggie observed, "but we
em to be the only ones who have made it here for breakfast."

"It's only eight o'clock," he replied, looking at his watch. Then,
nding toward Maggie, he lowered his voice. "Stella and Robert
dgeworthy are coming in," he whispered. Maggie glanced toward

the dining room entrance and waved. But Stella only gave her a wan smile before slipping into her seat.

"That is one very unhappy woman," Maggie said. "By the look of her, I doubt she had any sleep last night."

"If you're right and she knew nothing about the smuggling," Nat answered, "that little meeting in the lounge last night must have been a real eye-opener."

They were seated at their usual table overlooking the bay, and Maggie drew Nat's attention to a young man walking toward the lodge from the cabins near the bluff. "I'm sure that's one of the Smiths' sons," she said in a low voice. "He was in the emporium the day I was there." She thought for a moment. "Some biblical name . . . Noah, I think."

"Maggie," Nat said quietly, "Mahaffy said that the Smith brothers had captured Nancy. I wonder if that means they've brought her up here to the resort?"

"But why here? And if they have, where would they have hidden her?"

Nat shrugged. "Perhaps in one of the cabins?"

"But how can we find out?" Maggie asked worriedly as she arose from the table.

"At this point," Nat answered. "I haven't the foggiest idea." And he followed her out of the dining room.

"You survived the storm all right?" The receptionist—who also served as a waitress and barmaid—had just emerged from the kitchen carrying two coffee carafes.

"It's hard to believe that there was a storm," Maggie answered, "except that the power's still off and there's an awful mess piled up on the beach."

The receptionist nodded. "Just our luck when we have so many visitors. We even had three guys turn up by boat just after the storm broke. Damned lucky to make it at all."

"I think I saw one of them crossing the yard toward the lodge st now," Maggie said.

The receptionist nodded. "Yeah, probably coming in for eakfast. I had to put them in one of the cabins under the bluff. hose old cabins are pretty well ready to fall down, but at least it as a roof over their heads."

"You said there were three of them?" Nat asked.

"Yeah. One of them was so seasick they had to carry him the cabin. I asked if they needed a doctor, but they said they ould look after him."

"Which is their cabin?"

"The last one right next to the bluff," she nodded to the right the lodge, then left them to deliver her carafes of coffee.

When Nat and Maggie were halfway up the stairs, they anced down and saw Noah Smith below them, heading toward e dining room.

AT STOOD AT THEIR window and studied the three cabins stled in the trees at the base of the bluff. "I don't know if it will ork," he said at last, "but I've got an idea . . ."

A few minutes later, Maggie, with Oscar on his leash, walked urposefully out of the back door of the lodge and down the steps nto the path. She then turned right and walked until she met e narrow gravel road that served the three small cabins under e bluff. Oscar, straining on his leash, pulled her across the road ad straight into the closely growing alders and firs, and the thick ndergrowth of salmonberry bushes and sword ferns that grew ofusely around the cabins.

Nat leaned on the veranda railing and smoked a cigarette, aiting until Maggie and Oscar had disappeared among the foli- ;e before he discarded his butt in a sand bucket. Taking a quick ance around, he walked down to the pebble beach, where he picked up several seashells. Then, with head bent as though looking for more, he turned right and sauntered to the end of the beach, where creaming waves smashed against the huge boulders that met the base of the bluff.

Meanwhile, Maggie had pushed her way through the brush until she reached the back of the cabin nearest the cliff and peered into the small curtain-covered window. Then taking a chance, she rapped lightly on the glass. There was no response. *Perhaps she's tied up.* She rapped again. This time, the curtain moved slightly and Nancy's ravaged face appeared. Her mouth was taped and her eyes looked frightened and wild.

"We're going to get you out," Maggie mouthed.

Nancy nodded.

"Hey! Get away from that window!"

Maggie ducked down beneath the window, then scurried around the corner of the cabin to wave to Nat, who was waiting at the bottom of the bluff for her signal. He immediately clambered up from the beach and headed straight for the front door of the cabin.

"You got a brother having breakfast up at the lodge?" he asked the man who jerked the door open. He was probably in his early thirties, dressed in jeans and a grey sweatshirt, his unkempt hair matching his unshaved stubbly face.

"Why?"

"He said to tell you Mahaffy wants to see you in his cabin."

"Why didn't he come and tell me himself?" Job Smith asked suspiciously.

"He's eating his breakfast." Nat shrugged and started to turn away.

Job Smith looked up and down the empty side road. "Mahaffy told me he was going to come here."

"Change of plans. I wouldn't keep *that* man waiting if I was you." And Nat began sauntering off toward the beach again.

Job Smith hesitated, then emerged fully from the cabin, locked the door and walked rapidly toward the lodge, turning once or twice to make sure that Nat was not hanging around the cabin. As soon as he was out of sight, Nat ran back and within thirty seconds had picked open the lock.

"We've very little time," he told Nancy. Hauling her upright, he ripped the tape from her mouth, then quickly covered her mouth with his hand. "Don't make a sound." Kneeling on the floor, he started to grapple with the knots of the rope. But "the boys" had done too good a job. "Sit tight. I'll find a knife."

"Don't leave me, Nat. They're going to kill me."

"Shut up," he hissed as he pulled open kitchen drawers and began flinging out knives, forks and spoons.

Suddenly, Maggie yanked the door open. "For God's sake, let's get going." Oscar, with a deep-throated growl, strained at his leash to get to Nancy.

"Can't find a sharp knife," Nat yelled back.

"Take her into the woods. I'll find one."

Nat looked down at his slightly plump ex-wife. "There's nothing for it, Nancy," he said, yanking her to her feet. He slung her over his shoulder fireman-style and staggered out of the door.

Maggie dropped Oscar's leash and watched him scoot after Nat, then, rummaging in the drawers until she found a paring knife, grabbed it and raced after Nat, who was slashing his way through the thick underbrush. Oscar—dragging his leash and thinking this was a new kind of game—raced ahead of Maggie, jumping up and down as he tried to reach Nancy's bobbing head. When Maggie eventually caught up with them, she found Nat gasping for breath and leaning against a tree beside his ex-wife, whom he had unceremoniously dumped. Oscar, taking up his guard-dog stance, sat staring at her and growling deep in his throat.

"Get that animal away from me," Nancy demanded fearfully as Maggie knelt to start hacking at the bindings. "Oh oh! My legs are numb."

Maggie looked up at Nat. "We've got to get her to our room somehow."

"I've a better idea," he answered. "We'll get her into the back of the car."

"I'm cold," Nancy complained.

Maggie, taking no notice, hacked away until the ropes fell from Nancy's legs.

"There'll be a blanket on the back seat of the car. Come on," Nat added, pulling Nancy to her feet, "we've got to keep moving."

"What about my hands?"

"Here," Maggie said, handing Nat the knife. "You free her hands while I work my way nearer to the road to see if the coast is clear. No, Oscar. Stay with Nat." Nat and Nancy waited torturous minutes until Maggie returned with her finger to her mouth, indicating that they should be quiet.

"Mahaffy and the Smith brothers are marching down toward the cabin," she whispered. "We've got to work our way up through the trees and then be prepared to run across the road to the parking lot." And not waiting to see if they were following, she grabbed the dog's leash and moved as quickly as she could up the slope, pushing her way through the trees and bushes as she went, only stopping when she calculated she must be close to the parking lot.

"It's going to be tricky crossing the road without being seen," Nat whispered when he had regained his breath.

"I'll go first," Maggie answered, hoping that anybody seeing her would think she'd just been walking the dog. "I'll give you an okay signal if it's safe."

"I'm freezing," Nancy complained again.

"You'll be in a worse shape if the Smith brothers get you back," Maggie snapped. Not waiting for any more of Nancy's complaints, she walked briskly across the road and into the parking lot. "Oh damn!" she muttered. They didn't want any witnesses seeing them sneaking Nancy into Nat's car, and there was a deliveryman unloading crates of milk, eggs and cream from a small van and stacking them onto a dolly right opposite to where the car was parked. She stood behind the woodshed for what seemed an age before he returned to his vehicle and drove away. Maggie, quickly slipping back to the edge of the parking lot, gave them the okay signal. Now all it needed was Mahaffy and the Smiths to return to the lodge via the gravel road as they crossed.

"Can't we go up to your room?" a shivering Nancy whispered.

"Too risky," Nat whispered back as they reached the car. "Get in and cover yourself with the blanket." Then, turning to Maggie, he said, "Let's grab our bags and get out of here."

AFTER DRAGGING THEIR OVERNIGHT bags from the closet, they hurried to gather up items of clothing that had been left lying on chairs. They were just closing their bags when they heard a faint tapping on the door. Maggie looked at Nat inquiringly. "Who on earth can that be?"

"It can't be Mahaffy," he whispered. "He'd hammer on it."

They were still trying to decide whether they should answer it or not when there was another soft tap. Nat reached down and pulled the cord from the bedside lamp out of the wall plug, picked up the lamp and went to stand behind the door. Then he motioned for Maggie to open the door.

Stella Edgeworthy was standing uncertainly in the doorway. "I had to come and speak to you. I have to explain." Maggie could see that she been crying, and she was sporting a fresh shiner.

"Does your husband know you're here?" Maggie asked.

"He's with all the others in Schaefer's cabin. But I have to get back before he misses me."

"Come and sit down."

But instead, Stella walked over to the window, looked out and then paced back toward the door. "I didn't know what they were up to. You've got to believe me."

"But you must have realized something nasty was going on," Nat replied, taking a quick glance at his watch. "Especially after both Maurice and Jacquelyn were murdered."

"But that's what's so odd," she said. "They all deny killing them. And somehow I believe them."

"Then what was the object of them all meeting here at New Year's?"

"I'm such a fool. I really thought it was about buying a lot up here. But it turns out it was just a cover-up for a meeting of their smuggling ring."

"And you've only just found that out?" Nat asked in a disbelieving voice.

Stella nodded miserably. "But what I came to tell you was that when Robert told me to come and see you, he said I wasn't to tell you who else I saw here."

Nat frowned. "You mean besides your bunch?"

"Yes." Stella nodded. "He said I must have imagined seeing them . . . but I know I did . . ."

"Saw who?" Maggie asked.

"Maurice's kids."

"You saw René and Isabelle here at New Year's? Where?"

"Up near the entrance to the resort. There are some really old cabins up there."

"And you're sure that's who you saw?"

"Yes, I'm sure," Stella said, "even if Robert says I couldn't have."

She started for the door. "Anyhow, I just wanted you to know . . . I didn't mean to lie to you."

"Let's get out of here," Nat muttered as soon as the door closed behind Stella.

"If you can manage the bags and Oscar on your own," Maggie said, grabbing up her handbag, "I'll go down and turn in the key and settle up the bill. See you at the car."

"LEAVING US?" THE RECEPTIONIST asked, and then without waiting for a reply she continued, "We can sure use your room. I've already had to put a young couple who turned up this morning into one of the old cabins at the top of the property, and the only heat it's got is an ancient wood stove." She smiled. "At least the road's been cleared."

Thanking her, Maggie grabbed the receipt and headed for the door, then stopped. "How old did you say the couple were?"

"I didn't. But they're very young, especially the girl. Have a safe trip home." She turned to pick up the phone. "St Clare's Resort," she said into the receiver.

# CHAPTER EIGHTEEN

Just as Maggie reached the Chevy, a sudden movement near the lodge caught her eye, and she saw Mahaffy, the two Smith brothers and Schaefer coming around the corner of the building. "Oh! Blast!" And she quickly ducked behind the woodshed. She counted to one hundred before she risked taking a peek to see where the men were, then slid out of sight again as she heard Mahaffy call out, "Southby's old wreck is still parked over there, so they can't have taken her far."

"Do you want me to have a look?" one of the Smiths asked.

*Please say no!*

"Yeah! What the hell are you waiting for?"

Maggie held her breath and waited for them to discover Nancy in the car. But after a few minutes, she heard Noah Smith shout, "She's not here!" Finally, there was silence and she realized that the men must have gone into the lodge. Cautiously, Maggie emerged from her hiding place and opened the back door of the Chevy. No Nancy! Where the hell has she gone? "Nancy," she called in a hoarse whisper. Quickly she checked around the other cars in the parking lot. Still no sign of her. She retreated back to the woodshed to think. *I wonder,* she thought. *Could it be?* Fishing into her purse for a pad, she scrawled a note for Nat and left it on the dashboard. "Meet me at the entrance to the resort."

NAT PLACED BOTH BAGS in the hall, pulled the door closed and heard the lock snap behind him. Attaching the leash to the dog's collar, he asked, "Ready, Oscar?" The dog wagged his plume of a tail in answer.

At that moment, Mahaffy's voice floated up the main staircase. "We'll check their room first."

Bending down, Nat slung the strap of Maggie's bag over his shoulder, picked up the dog, and then, grabbing his own bag, ran down the corridor, frenziedly trying each doorknob. He had only seconds to spare as he slid into a steamy bathroom, turning the lock behind himself as he closed the door. Leaning his head against the door, he heard Mahaffy banging his fist on the door down the hall.

"What do you want, young man?" He turned to see an elderly lady sitting in the bath, fearfully clutching a towel to her ample breasts. "And what is that dog doing in here?"

"Oh, I'm so sorry," Nat answered. "I thought it was unoccupied."

"A person can't even get a bath in peace. And what's all that banging?"

Nat gave a little laugh. "Someone's trying to find me."

"I'm trying to have a bath and you're playing silly games," she said indignantly. "I'm going to complain to the management."

"Could that wait for a few minutes?" Nat pleaded. "It's very important those people don't find me."

She snorted. "You have a few minutes, young man. But please turn your back."

Nat obliged by turning around and putting his ear against the door to listen. Mahaffy seemed to have given up on the banging.

"They've gone," Job Smith called out.

"They can't have gone far," Mahaffy replied. "Try every door."

Watching the doorknob turning, Nat put his finger to his lips and mouthed a "please" to the elderly lady in the tub.

"It's locked," Smith said, giving the door a few mighty bangs.

Oscar, still in Nat's arms, gave a low growl. Nat quickly closed his hand over the dog's muzzle. "Quiet, quiet," he whispered. But the dog quivered when the second round of bangs resounded on the door and he gave a muffled bark. Then, to Nat's surprise, the old lady suddenly had a fit of exaggerated coughing.

"Open the door, you bastard!" Nat recognized Mahaffy's Irish drawl.

"Go away," the old lady shouted. "And please refrain from using that terrible language. I came in here for a soothing bath. Please be gone!"

There was a moment of shocked silence, then Smith said, "It's some woman in there."

"What's all this shouting?" an irate voice called out in the corridor. "What's going on?"

"I thought this was supposed to be a select resort," another voice answered.

"Sorry," Mahaffy answered. "Just a bit of fun."

"Well, keep it down."

Nat waited until everything was quiet, then, still keeping his eyes averted, said, "I would love to give you a great big kiss, but that would mean my turning around. Thank you." And opening the door, he and Oscar ran along the passageway and down the back stairs.

Peeping around the corner of the lodge, he saw the Smiths and Mahaffy conferring at the other end of the building. Waiting until they had disappeared, and holding tightly onto Oscar, who insisted on licking his face, he made a dash for his car, where he threw the squirming animal onto the back seat before diving behind the wheel and scrunching down.

"Nancy," he whispered. "Are you still there?"

There was no answer. He peeked over the back of the seat. No Nancy. It was only then that he noticed the note on the dashboard. "What the hell are they doing up at the gate?"

"FOR GOD'S SAKE! HOW much further is it to this damned lodge?" Patience was not Quentin De Meyer's strong point.

"Another three or four miles," George answered, signalling to make a left turn at the Garden Bay turnoff. "Cheer up and enjoy the scenery. You might even see some bears as we pass the dump."

"Bears! That's all I need."

# CHAPTER NINETEEN

M aggie shivered as she hurried up the steep road that led to the resort's main entrance. Near the gate she turned right onto the overgrown lane that led through scrub alders, clinging blackberry vines and salmonberry bushes that had grown unchecked for years. Looking down at her ruined stockings as she neared the cabin, she also wished she had taken the time to change from her tweed skirt into her warm wool slacks. The cabins, with their rusty corrugated roofs, cracked windows and broken porches, must have been the original buildings on the site. Parked outside the second one was an old army Jeep—a remnant of its camouflage paint still showing. She rapped on the door.

Isabelle opened the door. "I wondered how long it would be before you found us? You'd better come in." She stepped aside so that Maggie could see past her. Nancy, tied to a wooden chair, lifted her woebegone face and gave a wan smile. Beside her stood René, clutching a pair of iron fire tongs.

Maggie stepped inside and Isabelle slammed the door behind her. "There's no point in kidnapping this woman," Maggie said. "She doesn't know where the jewellery is!"

"She must know where it is," Isabelle snapped. "She stole it from the house."

Sadly, Nancy shook her head. "No, I didn't. I got it from

Robert Edgeworthy's office. He stole it from Jacquelyn."

"So where is it now?" René demanded.

"She buried it in her garden and somebody dug it up and took it," Maggie explained."

"I don't believe it," Isabelle said, and then turned to Nancy. "You buried that priceless stuff in your garden?"

"It's true," Nancy said sadly.

"Something is puzzling me," Maggie said. "Why didn't you tell me you were here when your father disappeared?"

René turned away, opened the door of the pot-bellied stove behind him and began poking at the feeble flames. "That wasn't any of your business."

"So why did you come back this weekend?"

"Because your secretary told me that the Smith brothers had grabbed the woman who stole Dad's Egyptian jewellery," René said.

"And that's why we know she's got it," Isabelle cut in. She pointed at Nancy, who shook her head sadly again.

"How did your father get the stuff in the first place?" Maggie asked. "Was he part of the smuggling ring?"

"No," René answered. "He found out what was going on, and I guess, knowing Dad, he demanded a payoff to keep quiet."

"He always called us his little family," Isabelle said vehemently, "but he was a blackmailer and a crook and a liar and then he got conned by that little gold digger." She turned to watch René ineffectually poking the reluctant fire. "Here, give them to me." And grabbing the tongs out of his hands, she bent down and pushed the pieces of wood into the flame.

"Isabelle," René said in a warning voice.

Ignoring him, she carried on, "He promised René a partnership in the logging business and then that Jacquelyn got him fired. And he was going to set me up with my own beauty salon."

"But why kill your own father?" Maggie asked softly.

Nancy stared at Maggie in horror. "You mean they killed Maurice?"

Isabelle stood up and turned from the fire to face Maggie. "Jacquelyn got him to change his will, and then she had the nerve to tell us that we had to stand on our own two feet." She laughed. "She said she and Dad were going to start their own family—if you can believe that!"

"Oh, Isabelle," René said sadly. "Why can't you keep your mouth shut?"

"I'd begun to figure it out for myself, anyway," Maggie told him. "And Jacquelyn? Did you kill her, too?"

"We had to," Isabelle answered. "With her gone, we inherit everything."

"Oh, my God, no," Nancy moaned. "Jacquelyn, too?"

"Oh, shut up," Isabelle snapped.

There was silence. Isabelle stood holding the tongs. She seemed to be daring Maggie to move.

"I guess we underestimated you," René said at last. "Your knowing all this changes everything."

"Nat knows that Nancy and I are here. And the police are on their way," Maggie answered, turning to walk towards the door.

Isabelle laughed. "I don't think so. Anyway, we'll have to take that chance."

Maggie was only a couple of feet away from the outside door and safety when she sensed a movement behind her. She ducked, but Isabelle was quicker, and the heavy iron fire tongs came crashing down on her head.

NAT SLOWLY PULLED HIMSELF up and peered in both directions before starting the engine and ramming the car into gear. He drove up the long, winding driveway to the entrance—no one was following—but he was sure that once Mahaffy saw that his car had gone, he would be hot on the chase. Nat hadn't realized how tense he was until the iron gates came into view and he began to breathe easier. *Now where the hell are you, Maggie?*

"Bloody hell!" A Jeep had suddenly appeared from the side road on the right and swerved directly toward him. Nat jammed on his brakes, shooting Oscar into the front seat. The Jeep didn't stop but kept going hell-bent for leather through the gates to disappear up the hill ahead. "Jesus!" Nat leaned his head on the steering wheel, his heart hammering.

"What's wrong, Oscar?" The dog was scrabbling frantically at the door. "Wait a sec." He leaned over and patted him on the head. "Let me park, okay?" Putting the car back into gear, he drove through the gates, but before he could pull over and park, a black Ford nosed its way toward them up the short, steep incline to the gates and halted beside him. Sergeant George Sawasky climbed out of his car.

Nat rolled down his window, and immediately Oscar leapt over him, out the window and raced up the hill.

"Oscar, come back here," Nat yelled.

"What's going on?" George asked.

"Maggie and Nancy are missing. She left a note telling me to meet her here at the gates."

Suddenly, George pointed back down the road. "My God, look!"

Nat climbed out of his car. "Nancy?"

They watched incredulously as Nancy, still tied to the wooden chair, hobbled toward them. "They've got Maggie," she shouted.

"Who has Maggie?" Nat said, running toward her.

"René and Isabelle! And they killed Maurice and Jacquelyn." And she sat down on the chair, tears running down her face. "Get me out of this, Nat," she pleaded.

Nat squatted down beside her and started to untie the ropes.

At that moment, the passenger door of George's car opened and out popped Quentin De Meyer. "I've got to get down to the resort before the Coast Guard arrives," he yelled. "Can't you catch up on your social life later?"

"Take the damned car, Quentin," George yelled back. "I'm going to help Nat find Maggie. Now," he continued, pulling Nancy free from her chair, "let's follow Oscar. He knows where she's gone." Grabbing Nancy by the arm, George helped her toward Nat's car.

Nat slid behind the wheel, and moments later the old Chevy was heading up the hill in the direction that Oscar had gone.

"Let's get away from this goddamned place," Nancy screamed from the back seat.

"But I only saw two people in that Jeep," Nat said as he drove.

"They probably threw her in the back," Nancy chimed in. "Isabelle hit her on the head and she was out cold."

"Oh, my God!" Nat groaned. "I can't believe those two are murderers."

"That's one of the reasons I'm here," George said, holding tightly to the door handle as Nat pushed his foot down on the accelerator. "Scene of crime officers have finally identified two distinct sets of fingerprints in places that only the killer or killers could have left them. And Jacquelyn's maid told us that René had become a frequent visitor since Maurice's death. And on that particular night, she had helped Jacquelyn prepare dinner for the two of them."

"René?" Nat asked in disbelief.

"And the other prints were Isabelle's. Let's hope we can catch up to them."

"And Maggie must have figured it out," Nat answered grimly. "But where could they be going?"

## CHAPTER TWENTY

Maggie could hear somebody moaning, and as she struggled to wake up, she realized that the moaning was coming from her. All she wanted to do was sink back into sleep, but subconsciously she knew that she must wake up. *Okay. I'm in a car of some sort and I've hurt my head. Whose car?* She tried hard to think. Then it came to her—she was lying in a fetal position on the floor behind the front seats of a car. *It's René's Jeep!*

"I hope you didn't kill her," Maggie heard René say.

"What's it matter?" the girl answered. "We have to get rid of her anyway."

"I can't do it, Isabelle."

Maggie realized the car had stopped.

"Keep going, you idiot," his stepsister ordered him.

*I must pull myself together*, Maggie thought. She tried to flex her legs without the two in front seeing the movement.

René rammed the Jeep into gear and turned right. Maggie had to stifle a cry of pain as the Jeep's acceleration caused her head to strike the hard metal floor.

"There's a big lake at the end of this road," Isabelle said, glancing over her shoulder to check on Maggie.

"So?" René asked.

"That's where we dump her."

"No! We've done enough killing, Isabelle," René answered.

"You're a big baby, René," she sneered. "Baby!"

NAT TURNED RIGHT AT the crest of the hill onto Hotel Lake Road and drove around the twists and turns until he was skirting the lake itself.

"There's a turnoff ahead," George yelled.

"Which way would they have gone?"

"Go right," George shouted. "Look! Skid marks."

Nat rammed the old car into gear and tore around the corner, but the tires hitting the muddy verge caused the car to begin a slow skid and head straight for the lake's edge. He yanked hard on the steering wheel, but the car was slow to respond and continued its slide across the mud. There was nothing he could do but hold onto the wheel. Gradually, the vehicle stopped skidding and came to rest a mere foot away from the lapping water.

"For God's sake," Nancy yelled. "You nearly got us killed!"

Nat took a few deep breaths, then carefully reversed back onto the gravel road. "Sorry about that," he said in a very shaky voice.

"This is just a wild goose chase," Nancy continued to yell at him. "We'll never catch up to them."

"Look," George yelled. "There's Oscar!"

Nat didn't bother to answer as he pulled up beside the tired little dog, opened the door and scooped him up. "Good boy, Oscar. You're a real hero!" And they continued the chase.

MAGGIE FELT THE JEEP'S speed easing off and knew that they must be nearing the lake where the two of them were proposing to dump her. But not without a fight, she thought. She took a few deep breaths to clear her aching head as she watched the driver's loose seat sliding back and forth on its metal runners.

"There!" Isabelle yelled. "Pull off under those trees." She glanced over her shoulder. "Hurry up, she's coming around. I'll have to give her another bang on the head when we stop. The water will do the rest."

From her position on the Jeep's floor, Maggie was unable to see ahead, so had to wait until she felt the car beginning to make the turn. She pulled her legs up even closer to her body until her knees were against the back of René's broken seat. Taking a deep breath, she pushed with all her strength. The sudden jolt slammed René into the steering wheel. The Jeep, now out of control and fishtailing in the loose gravel, skidded sideways into a huge rock, the passenger door flew open with the impact, and Isabelle was flung out onto the grass. Maggie found herself flying backwards. And then, by sheer willpower, she pulled herself over the back of the Jeep to collapse onto the ground, where comforting blackness took over.

"TAKE IT EASY. THERE'S a sharp bend ahead."

"And skid marks going straight for the lake!" Nat said.

"It's the Jeep!" George shouted.

"Where's Maggie?" Nat cried out in anguish.

"What's she doing?" Nancy yelled.

Nat jammed his foot on the brake and brought the Chevy to a shuddering stop. He flung the car door open and raced towards Isabelle, who, holding a large rock, was bending over Maggie.

But René got there faster. "Isabelle, no-o-o!" he was screaming as he lunged at his stepsister. The girl looked up in surprise as his body hurtled toward her, and the next second she was flying backwards into the cold waters of the lake.

"Maggie, Maggie!" Nat, kneeling beside her, took her into his arms. "If you've killed her . . ." he threatened René.

"I'm sorry," René said. "But I wouldn't have let Isabelle kill her."

George knelt and felt for Maggie's pulse. "We've got to get her to a hospital. There's one just down the road—we passed a sign pointing to it on the way up here."

"You stay and help George with those two," Nancy said firmly as she covered Maggie with the blanket from Nat's car. "I'll take the car and go for help."

"Okay," George said and looked toward the lake. "I'd better fish that girl out of the water before she drowns."

"Oh, for God's sake, let her drown," Nancy said as she tried to stop Oscar licking Maggie's face.

Nat, looking down at the sleeve of his jacket, realized that it was soaked in blood—then he saw the gaping wound on the back of her head. Gathering her up in his arms, he staggered to the car and placed her gently on the back seat.

Suddenly, Nancy pushed him aside, lifted the blanket again and started removing Maggie's shoes.

"Why are you taking her shoes off?"

"Can't drive in bare feet, can I?" she answered as she crushed her feet into Maggie's pumps and began climbing into the driver's seat of the Chevy. "Now get over there and help drag that miserable little bitch out of the water."

"But I must go with Maggie!"

"No," Nancy said firmly. "Go and help George. I'm quite capable—in case you've forgotten!"

Nat looked to where George was trying to haul a dripping Isabelle out of the water. "Okay," he answered reluctantly, closing the back door of the car. "Just carry on down this road to Garden Bay Lake and . . ." But Nancy had rammed the Chevy into gear and was already out of earshot.

It was a good hour later before she returned, suitably backed up with an RCMP officer, to find that Isabelle—shivering with the cold, but still looking defiant—and her brother had been handcuffed and were sitting back to back on the ground, waiting.

# CHAPTER TWENTY-ONE

It was a week since Maggie had been transferred from Garden Bay Hospital on the Sunshine Coast to a private room in St. Paul's in Vancouver. Although she still wore a turban bandage covering most of her head, the bruises had faded to dull yellows and purples, and the cuts were healing nicely.

"I hear you are having a few visitors this evening," the nurse said after removing Maggie's supper tray. "Remember what Dr. Dryfus said—don't get too tired. Just shoo them out when you've had enough."

Maggie nodded obediently, knowing full well she couldn't wait to hear all the news from Nat, George and Quentin.

But it was Henny who arrived first, though she was followed closely by Nat, who leaned over to gently gather Maggie into his arms. She was sure he looked a lot older than when she had last seen him. "I'm okay, Nat," she reassured him. "I'm okay. But is Nancy all right?"

"She's fine. But a little subdued. Some day I'll tell you how she helped rescue you."

"Here," Henny said, thrusting a small cardboard box at Maggie. "They make bad food in hospital."

Maggie carefully undid the knots of the butcher string and opened the lid of the box. "How nice of you," she said, trying not ɔ laugh. Inside were six very large, lumpy Henny specials.

Henny beamed. "Ja. Mr. Nat said I could come and hear ergeant George tell what happened."

As if on cue, the door opened and George crept in with a ouquet of daffodils and tulips. "Thought some spring flowers ʳould cheer you up," he said, bending down and giving her a peck n the cheek. "You're not too tired for us?"

"No. I'm dying to hear all the details. Is Quentin coming, ɔo?"

"He sends his regrets. Had to fly to Egypt to tie up the loose nds there, hopefully before they realize that the Vancouver end f their operation has dried up. But not to worry—he said it's kay for me to tell you all about the smuggling ring." He pulled chair up close to the bed. "As we had surmised," he began, "it ll started during the war, when Schaefer's unit was in Egypt. Henry Smith was his quartermaster and deep into the black ɲarket that was rife at that time. It didn't take him long to dis-ɔver that there were stolen antiquities for the asking."

"Were they all stolen from the tombs?" Nat asked.

George shook his head. "Not all. Some were from museums, ᵖrivate collections, or wherever the thieves could get their hands ᵒn them. Anyway, Smith knew that Lieutenant Liam Mahaffy ᵥasn't above a little bit of larceny. He recognized the possibilities ᵒf the scheme and decided to let his friends Colonel Schaefer and Lieutenant Edgeworthy into the plan. It grew from there."

"Did they meet Bakhash in Egypt?" Nat asked.

"No." George explained, "He and his wife were already living ɲ Vancouver. It was Sharifa Bakhash's brother who was Smith's ɔontact man in Egypt. Her family own acres of flax fields and ᵗhe mill to process the linen, as well as several fabric stores," he ᵈded, "and they were already into smuggling—though in a much ɲaller way."

"So it got going in earnest when the war was over?" Maggie asked.

"Yes. Edgeworthy and Schaefer both lived in Vancouver, and Schaefer sponsored Mahaffy so he could immigrate. The Smith family followed soon after."

"They needed the Smiths' emporium to move the goods," Nat interjected.

"Yes," George agreed.

"It is like a movie," Henny said, moving her chair closer.

George smiled at her. "It didn't take them too long to get into full swing. Bakhash would order his fabric from his brother-in-law and he would pack the stolen stuff into the hollow cardboard sleeves."

"And René and I saw them emptying the stuff out of the sleeves," Maggie said.

"And Maurice Dubois?" Nat asked. "How did he get into it?"

"Ah! He was the fly in the ointment. Somehow he found out about the smuggling through working with Schaefer—hence his nice little blackmail scheme. The antiquities he got were payment for his silence."

"No wonder the gang wanted to retrieve them from his house," Maggie said, leaning back on her pillows.

Nat reached for her hand. "Are we tiring you too much?"

Maggie shook her head. "I'm fine. Go on, George."

"Maurice Dubois's death was a gift from heaven for the gang, and as soon as he was out of the way, Edgeworthy was given the job of getting the stuff back." He chuckled. "Of course, he was the real estate agent who had sold the house to Dubois in the first place."

"So he still had a key?" Henny asked.

George nodded.

"And then Nancy found the stuff in Edgeworthy's office." Na

looked pensive. "But what I don't get is how they disappeared from Nancy's backyard. And who got them?"

George shook his head. "No. That's still a mystery. Nancy is absolutely adamant that she buried them under the birdbath, and the smuggling gang are just as adamant that they dug the whole place up and the stuff wasn't there."

"When did you begin to suspect René and Isabelle?" George asked Maggie.

Maggie thought for a moment before answering. "I couldn't for the life of me see why, once the gang had got the stuff back from Jacquelyn, there was any need to kill her."

"That puzzled me, too," George agreed. "She seemed very young and naïve when I questioned her on her husband's murder. I'm sure she wanted to believe he'd bought the antiquities legitimately."

"So if she knew nothing about the smuggling ring," Nat cut in, "she was no threat to them."

"That's precisely why I couldn't fathom why they would kill her," Maggie said. "But it was a very long time before I suspected Maurice's kids, because René seemed so genuine and Isabelle was so young."

"But René was such a nice boy," Henny said sadly.

Maggie said slowly, "You know, I couldn't see René as a killer either. I'm sure Isabelle was the mastermind behind both murders. René just couldn't stand up to her."

"Yes, we're positive that the girl did the actual murders," George conceded. "But René did nothing to stop her, so he's being charged as an accomplice."

"It was the rings that worried me," Maggie continued.

"What rings?" Henny said, leaning forward.

"Jacquelyn's rings. When she came to our office, her hands were covered in very expensive rings—and I'm sure every one of them was genuine."

"So?" Nat asked.

"I couldn't help but notice that Isabelle was also wearing masses of rings when she and René came to ask us to carry on with the investigation. Of course," she added, "I couldn't swear they were Jacquelyn's, but where else would Isabelle have got them, other than by stealing them from Jacquelyn? She and her mother have no money."

"You're right about Jacquelyn's jewellery," George said. "They were the only things missing when she was killed. We figured that the killer took the jewels to make the murder look like a botched break and entry."

"You said that both René's and Isabelle's fingerprints were found in the house," Nat said.

"Isabelle's were left on the glass-topped dressing table in the bedroom—probably when she stole the jewels. René left a bloody fingerprint on the back of the wooden headboard."

"What did they say when you confronted them on the two murders?"

"René said that he was sitting and talking to his father on the beach at the resort, when Isabelle came up behind and hit Maurice on the head with a rock. They panicked when they saw that he was dead, put him in the back of the Jeep, covered him with a blanket and headed straight back home."

"And Jacquelyn?" Nat asked.

"René and Jacquelyn had been having an affair for quite a few months—as you know, they were about the same age. But on the night of the murder, Isabelle had followed him to the house and hidden in one of the rooms until they were in bed together. She had simply walked in on them and stabbed her stepmother to death."

"And he let her do it?" Maggie exclaimed, horrified.

"I asked the same question," George answered. "René said

there was no stopping her. She just went berserk. He sobbed when he related the story, because he said he loved Jacquelyn and he had no idea that Isabelle would murder her. The girl's a nutcase, and I think she was very jealous of Jacquelyn."

"So," Henny said slowly, "you mean René and Jacquelyn were ... were ..."

They all nodded and Nat said, "They were lovers."

"But she was his stepmother!" Henny said in a shocked voice.

"They weren't blood relatives, Henny," Nat explained. "And as George said, they were very close in age. And of course, Maurice Dubois was very dead, so technically she wasn't even his stepmother anymore."

"Why did they leave Maurice's body on the mountain?" Henny asked suddenly.

"To give themselves time. They figured that everyone at the lodge would think Maurice had gone off somewhere on his own. They hoped that it would take a while before they realized that he was really missing and would start to look for him. We think that René was the one who thought of Hollyburn Mountain."

"Ah, yes," Nat said slowly. "He did tell us that he'd worked briefly on the clear-cutting up there."

"But how on earth did they manage to get the body so high up the mountain?" Maggie asked.

"Used a sled. After all, they are both very young and very fit. It was just bad luck for them that Maggie stumbled on the body so soon after they bury him with twigs and snow."

"I'm curious about one thing," Nat said. "Would their father's estate have come to them on Jacquelyn's death?"

"No," George said, getting to his feet. "Apart from a few bequests, Maurice Dubois left his entire estate to Jacquelyn, and she in turn left it all to a younger sister in Montreal."

"So the murders were for nothing," Henny said.

"What about Stella Edgeworthy?" Maggie asked. "She swore that she knew nothing about her husband's activities. In fact, although she put on a brave front, I think she's very frightened of him."

"She must've had some inkling what he was up to," George answered. "Anyway, she's been allowed to go home on bail."

"George, I haven't really thanked you for helping Nat to rescue me," Maggie said. "You always come through for us."

"That's what friends are for, Maggie," he said.

At this point, the door opened and the nurse came tut-tutting in. "Mrs. Spencer must have her rest," she said, tapping the watch pinned to her uniform.

"We're just leaving," George said contritely.

"I'll be in tomorrow," Nat promised as he bent to kiss her. "Anything you want?"

Maggie shook her head. "Only to get out of this place and into my own bed," she whispered. "How are Oscar and Emily doing without me?" she asked plaintively.

"They miss you. But you'll be home soon."

MAGGIE LAY BACK ON her pillows after they had left and went through everything again in her mind. A slight noise at the door made her look up, and there was Midge holding a huge basket of fruit in her arms. Jason was standing behind her.

"Your nurse said you're very tired as you've had a lot of visitors," Midge said as she placed the basket on the table. "So we promised we would only stay a minute or two."

"It is so lovely to see you both." Maggie suddenly found herself very weepy. "Sorry. I guess I *am* a bit tired."

"We have some news for you," Midge said as she handed her mother a tissue. "And you are the very first in the family to hear it." Pulling her left glove off, she extended her hand to Maggie. "I'm putting this poor man out of his misery. We're engaged."

"Oh, how wonderful. Here, help me to sit up so I can see the ring properly. So when is the big wedding day?"

"I don't want to wait too long," Jason said, sitting down on the end of the bed, "in case she changes her mind again. So we're going to do it in June."

"Yes," bubbled Midge. "I know Barbara is going to be mad as hell because she will be as big as a house by then—but what the heck; we don't want to wait."

"And I can't wait to get out of here and help you shop for your trousseau," Maggie said impatiently.

"That's another bit of news I got for you," Midge said. "I've spoken to Dr. Dryfus, and after I told him that I was taking time off to look after you when you leave here, he agreed that if you continue to improve, he will let you go home by the end of the week."

"Oh, thank you, darling! Thank you. Nat will be pleased," Maggie said.

"Yeah!" Jason said, smiling. "I think he's fed up with having to look after your house, as well as Oscar and Emily, and coping single-handed at the agency. He told me that the dog's moping for you, and that your 'damned cat' has a mind of her own."

"Well," Maggie replied, smiling, "at least he does have Henny to look after him at the office."

"I've heard about her wonderful cookies," Midge said.

"Here. Have one." Maggie reached over to her side table. "You are very welcome," she added, laughing.

After they had left, Maggie lay back on her pillows, already planning a June wedding and wondering what she would wear.

# EPILOGUE

Mrs. Mable Maggs hid behind the curtains in her back bedroom and watched her odd neighbour, Mrs. Gladstone, raking the earth around the concrete birdbath in her back garden.

"Never gives up, I must say that for the woman." Letting the lace curtain drop, she left the room and walked along the passage to her own bedroom. There, she lowered the Venetian blinds, pulled the top drawer of her dressing table open and carefully lifted out a musical jewellery box with a dancing figurine on the lid. Her late husband, Albert, had given it to her on one of her birthdays—she couldn't remember which.

She opened the lid, and the music tinkled.

She lifted the silver earrings out of the box and fastened them to the drooping lobes of her ears. Then, turning her head this way and that, she watched the earrings swing and glitter in her mirrored reflection. An ornate necklace followed next, and after placing it around her wrinkled neck, she preened again. It was fashioned out of the same silver, turquoise and tiny blue beads as the earrings and one of the bracelets—all very pretty, but all very heavy. The bangles were much lighter, as they seemed to be made of some kind of wood, but they were far too big for her wrinkled arms. Finally, she pushed two jewelled combs into her wispy grey hair. She couldn't for the life of her think what the funny little carved stones were for—they were too small to put into her rockery—but the grandkids would enjoy playing with them.

"So what do you think of me now, Albert?" she asked the black and white photograph of her late husband. It was a shame she couldn't show the stuff off to her cronies when she went to play bingo that afternoon. "Ah, well," she sighed. She'd keep them until her odd neighbour stopped looking for them in her backyard, and then she'd take the whole lot along to Mr. Steinway's pawnshop and see what he would give her for them.

Even though they followed the directions they had been given, it was after eight before Maggie and Nat found the old house on William Street. Badly in need of a paint and repair job, even the front porch listed to one side. It looked dark and deserted.

"No lights," Maggie said with a shiver.

"Perhaps he likes sitting in the dark. Come on." But after repeated knockings, there was still no answer. "Let's try the back."

"You go first," Maggie said nervously. "It's your idea." She couldn't see anything attractive about the house—a large square box sitting on a double lot, walls covered in grey, weather-beaten shingles, sash windows on either side of the front door, and three more on the second floor—a dismal place. The light was fading fast, but they could still see an unkempt backyard overgrown with blackberry vines, thistles and dandelions. "Nat!" she said suddenly, tapping him on the shoulder, "Over there. Looks like some kind of barn."

"Fairly new, too," he answered. The tall, wooden building seemed to loom at them out of the dusk. "Can't be a garage," he continued. "There's no street access and there seems to be only one door."

"But why such large windows?"

"I'll knock on the back door of the house, and if he doesn't answer, we'll go over and have a peek." He lifted his fist and banged hard on the door. "That's odd, it's open." Poking his head inside, he yelled, "Sheldon! Sheldon! Anyone home?"

"It's no good, Nat," Maggie said, tugging at his jacket. "He's obviously out. Let's go."

"I'll just have a quick look inside."

"No. That's trespassing." She stopped for a moment. "What's that terrible smell?"

"Garbage?" he said hopefully.

"Please let's get out of here."

But Nat had pushed the door open wider and entered into a mudroom that contained a wringer washer, a laundry tub, and shelves with cans and jars of food. Pushing through shirts, pajamas, underwear and socks draped dejectedly from a wooden clothes dryer hanging from the ceiling, he opened an adjoining door and flicked on a light that revealed a surprisingly clean kitchen. "Come on, Maggie," he called back to her.

"I don't like this, Nat," she said when she had joined him. "Call again, and then let's go home."

"Sheldon," he yelled again. Turning to Maggie, he said, "Why don't you have a quick look around down here while I go upstairs and make sure he isn't ill or something." Not waiting for her reply, he strode through the dark hallway and disappeared up a flight of carpeted stairs.

Maggie watched him ascend, then turned back into the kitchen and opened the door into a sparsely furnished dining room. Her face wrinkled with distaste when she saw the plate of congealed eggs, shriveled bacon and a half-eaten slice of toast. In front of the plate, propped against a bottle of ketchup, was an open book of illustrated paintings. A wooden chair had been pushed back from the table and lay on its side. "Seems he left in a hurry, so what scared him?" she asked the empty room.

Closing the door, she walked back through the kitchen and into the hall and stood at the foot of the stairs. "You okay, Nat?" But all she could hear were the creaking floorboards as he went from room to room. Can't wait to get out of this spooky place. She turned the white and blue porcelain doorknob to the last room on the ground floor and gasped when a musty smell rushed out to meet her. Taking a deep breath, she fumbled on the wall until she found a switch, but the light from the dusty chandelier did little to enhance the Victorian parlour. Red velvet drapes covered the window, solid oak furniture, bric-a-brac displayed on a wicker stand, overstuffed sofa and armchairs, everything covered in a patina of dust. But Maggie found herself drawn to a large oil painting set over the marble mantle piece. It was of an elderly, prim woman, not even a hint of a smile on her sharp features. She was wearing a white lace mobcap—and her beady black eyes followed Maggie's every move. Maggie quickly turned and rushed out of the room, pulling the door firmly behind her.

"I'm going outside," she called to Nat. "I need some air." She didn't wait for his reply, but continued out through the kitchen and mudroom into the backyard. But even the fresh air seemed tainted.

The moon had now risen and was casting long shadows over the backyard and the barn-like structure at the end of the garden. Taking her flashlight out of her pocket, she walked slowly down the cement path that led to the entrance of the building, but it took her several minutes to lift the heavy wooden hasp fastening the door before she could step inside.

The smell! That tell tale smell. Pulling her scarf from around her neck, she held it over her mouth and nose while she used her flashlight to locate a light switch.

At first she thought it was red paint. But as she got closer, she saw it was blood. Blood from the man's throat, which had been slit from ear to ear. Her first gut feeling was to turn tail and flee from the place, but forcing herself not to gag, she took another look. "Oh! Blast! Why is it always me that has to find them?" The corpse had been arranged artistically on a chaise lounge set on a dais, and a dozen or more easels had been placed in a circle around the dais, as if waiting for the lesson to begin.

Maggie, holding the scarf over her mouth, stumbled out of the studio just as Nat came out of the house.

"There you are," he said. "I've been calling you."

"In there," she answered in a shaky voice.

"What's in there?"

"He's . . . he's dead."

"Who's dead?"

"Go and see for yourself."

"Bloody hell!" he said a short time later as he shut the door behind him. "You do find them, don't you, Maggie?" Walking to where she was standing, he pulled her into his arms and held her close. "Come on, let's get to a telephone."

"At least we know what the building is used for," she laughed shakily.

"Apart from the dead body, I'd say it's a very fancy art studio."

They waited in front of the house for the first patrol car to turn up.

"You the one called in about a dead man?" The veteran officer asked as he climbed out of the car, followed by a baby-faced younger cop.

Nat nodded. "Around the back." He led the way.

"Holy Shit!" the senior officer exclaimed from the doorway of the studio a few minutes later. "You haven't touched anything?"

Nat shook his head.

"Call into the station and tell them it's homicide," the officer said to his green-in-the-gills partner. "And I'll talk to you and your wife in the kitchen."

"You know the dead man?" Officer O'Grady asked.

"He's an employee of a client of ours." Nat answered, handing over one of their cards.

"Private investigator! So what were you investigating?"

"His employer was worried because he hadn't turned up for work."

"And you were hired to find him?"

"No," Maggie answered. "He's part of a major investigation."

"And you are . . . ?"

"Margaret Spencer. The other name on that card."

"So what are you and the . . . ahem . . . lady investigator investigating?" he asked with a smirk.

"Murder," Maggie answered curtly. "Murder."

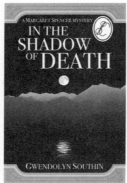
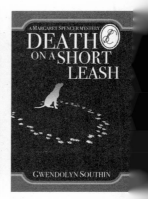

## INTRODUCING THE LULU MALONE
## MYSTERY SERIES

A gutsy new detective series, The Lulu Malone Mysteries present meditations on the life of the artist, in between muggings, murders and mayhem.

"Unlikely heroine Lulu Malone delivers a sweet serving of just desserts to a curious cast of bad guys in the sprightly Deadly Dues. With killer dimples, and friends to match, adorable Lulu charmingly stumbles her way through a whodunit romp. Linda Kupecek shows great promise with an eye for gloriously ridiculous situation comedy mixed with whimsy."—Anthony Bidulka, author of the Russell Quant mystery series

**Deadly Dues**
978-1-894898-98-0
$12.95, softcover

---

Recently released *Never Sleep with A Suspect on Gabriola Island*, the first in a new series by power-duo Sandy Frances Duncan and George Szanto

*Always Kiss the Corpse*
COMING Fall 2010

"An exciting adventure that readers will find entertaining, well-written and a solid foundation for future episodes in the Islands Investigations International series."—*Mysterious Reviews*

"Authors Sandy Duncan and George Szanto have written a seamless mystery that sparkles with a sense of place and a pair of reluctant private investigators who are not short of a foible or two."—*The Hamilton Spectator*

**Never Sleep with a Suspect on Gabriola Island**
978-1-894898-89-8
$14.95, softcover

GWENDOLYN SOUTHIN WAS BORN in Essex, England, and launched her career after moving to the Sunshine Coast of Canada. She co-founded The Festival of the Written Arts and the region's writer-in-residence program. She co-edited *The Great Canadian Cookbook* with Betty Keller, and her short stories and articles have appeared in *Maturity, Pioneer News* and *Sparks from the Forge*. She is at work on more Margaret Spencer adventures and lives in Sechelt, British Columbia.